Henry Bathurst Hanna

Backwards or Forwards?

Henry Bathurst Hanna

Backwards or Forwards?

ISBN/EAN: 9783337368371

Printed in Europe, USA, Canada, Australia, Japan

Cover: Foto ©Andreas Hilbeck / pixelio.de

More available books at **www.hansebooks.com**

INDIAN PROBLEMS

NO. III

Backwards or Forwards?

BY

COLONEL H. B. HANNA

FORMERLY BELONGING TO THE PUNJAUB FRONTIER
FORCE AND LATE COMMANDING AT DELHI
AUTHOR OF "CAN RUSSIA INVADE
INDIA?" AND "INDIA'S SCIENTIFIC
FRONTIER"

" As to holding Afghanistan, it would be folly equalling that of the attempt to
conquer it."—*Sir Charles Napier.*
" Triumph you may ; confident you may be, as I am, in the gallantry of your
troops ; but when through your gallantries the victory has been gained,
and you have succeeded, then will come your difficulties."—*The
Duke of Wellington on The Invasion of Afghanistan*

MAP Military and Commercial Railways on the North-West
Frontier at end of volume

WESTMINSTER
ARCHIBALD CONSTABLE AND COMPANY
2 WHITEHALL GARDENS S.W
And at all Booksellers

CONTENTS

PAGE

PREFACE vii

CHAPTER I

FRONTIER FORTIFICATIONS 1

CHAPTER II

MILITARY RAILWAYS 17

CHAPTER III

COST OF THE FORWARD POLICY 41

CHAPTER IV

RUSSIA'S POSITION IN CENTRAL ASIA . . . 80

CHAPTER V

THE ALTERNATIVES 109

" There will be no Russian invasion of India. . . . Russia has long under-stood both our strength and our weakness. There will be no foolish raid as long as India is united in tranquillity and contentment under British rule. Russia well knows that such an attempt would only end in the entire destruction of the invaders. . . . The danger then is imaginary. Herat is no more the key to India than is Tabreez, or Khiva, or Kokand, or Meshed. . . . No, the dream is idle : England's dangers are in India, not without ; and we trust that it will be in India they will be met, and that there will be no third Afghan campaign. Such a move would be playing Russia's game. We are safe while we hold our ground and do our duty " *Sir Henry Lawrence, in* 1856

" So far as the invasion of India in that quarter, it is the opinion of Her Majesty's Government that it is hardly practicable. The base of operations of any possible foe is so remote, the communications are so difficult, the aspect of the country so forbidding, that we have long arrived at the opinion that an in-vasion of our Empire, by passing the mountains which form our North-West frontier, is one which we need not dread "

Lord Beaconsfield, Speech on Lord Mayor's Day, 1878

PREFACE

IN the eighteen months which have elapsed since the first of my Indian Problems—*Can Russia Invade India?*—saw the light, a marked change has come over the tone of many English newspapers, even those which still cling to the Forward Policy, seeming anxious to clear themselves of all suspicion of belief in the possibility of a Russian Invasion of India. I will not inquire how much of this change is due to the persistency with which I have striven to drive the geographical, climatic, transport, and commissariat facts that rule the military situation in Central Asia, both for Russia and for ourselves, into the mind of the British Public, but simply hail it as the first step towards the acceptance of the views which find their final expression in the present volume.

Since the publication of my second Indian Problem—*India's Scientific Frontier: Where Is It? What Is It?*—a change of even greater imme-

diate importance must have passed over the views
of the Military Authorities in India; for, unless
the newspapers of that country are strangely mis-
informed, they have opened their eyes to the
weakness of their dispositions in the vast regions
lying between India's natural and political frontiers—that weakness which I had exposed and
denounced—and are trying to remedy it by drawing in their scattered troops, and handing over a
number of outlying posts to the care of tribal
levies. They have only to persist in this reasonable course to find themselves, at last, without
any violent catastrophe, any humiliating yielding
to compulsion, safe once more within the invulnerable frontier, to which in the following pages
I have invited them to return.

Throughout the entire work of which this
volume is the concluding instalment, I have
spoken of Russia as of a foe. My argument required that I should take this view of her; it is
the true view, so long as we hold to a policy
which compels her to see an enemy in ourselves.
But once erase India from the list of subjects over
which we may some day quarrel, once convince
her that we have learnt to view the expansion of

her power in Central Asia without jealousy and
without fear, and the ground will be cleared for
the establishment of a better understanding between her and ourselves ; and certainly I count
the opportunity of approaching all points of difference that exist, or may arise between us, in a
calmer and more generous spirit than is possible
to-day, as not the least of the gains to be put to
the credit of both nations, when the Forward
Policy has finally been abandoned on each side
of the Hindu Kush.

                                    H. B. HANNA.

October 10th, 1896.
  JUNIOR ARMY AND NAVY CLUB,
    ST. JAMES'S STREET, S.W.

P.S. — While these pages have been going
through the press, events have been happening
which enforce their arguments and point their
moral. On the one hand, we have in India a
widespread scarcity which may develop into a
famine greater than that of 1876–77 ; on the other
hand, the raids of the Maris on the Bolan Railway.

The Indian Government is taking credit to itself for its readiness to meet the distress, and
British newspapers are congratulating India upon

the irrigation works, which have lessened the area within which her crops are at the mercy of a rainless season, and upon the railways, which enable the surplus products of one district to be rapidly transferred to another; but how much greater cause there might have been for gratulation and self-gratulation if the millions which have been spent upon military lines running through uninhabited wastes, and on fortifications which defend nothing except the troops that they enclose, had gone in the multiplication of irrigation canals and commercial railways, and the improvement of country roads !

When the Central Government of India confessed that its demands upon the exchequers of the Provincial Governments had deprived the latter of the power to develop the vast territories under their charge, it was mainly works which help to prevent famine that it had in its mind ; and its own confiscation of Rs. 70,000,000 of the fund set apart for this specific purpose has contributed to intensify the misery which it will now have to mitigate at an enormous cost, and with no perceptible profit to the State, for relief works are, proverbially, wasteful and useless.

As for the murder of workmen and officials on the Bolan Railways, such incidents—common enough, if the truth were known—are the natural fruit of the military position, for which we have to thank the Forward School of politicians.

Shut up in scattered forts, in the midst of a population Afghan enough to dislike us the more, the more they see of us,[1] the so-called garrison of Beluchistan is little better than an imprisoned force, each unit of which is barely strong enough for its own defence, whilst its whole strength and influence, confessedly inadequate for the protection of travellers, prove to be also unequal to the duty of guaranteeing the lives of the civil population engaged in the arduous task of keeping open its communications with India.

---

[1] "It may not be very flattering to our *amour propre*, but I feel sure I am right when I say, *that the less the Afghans see of us, the less they will dislike us.*"—Sir Frederick (*now* Lord) Roberts' Memorandum, dated Kabul, 29th May, 1880.

BACKWARDS OR FORWARDS?

CHAPTER I

FRONTIER FORTIFICATIONS

" Fortresses so much in advance of the main territories and strength of a country, add neither to the offensive nor defensive powers of a state, but compromise a certain portion of its strength in men and means by isolating them at vast distances from support in the midst of a hostile country." — GENERAL SIR HENRY DURAND, *Royal Engineers.*

" A large fort requires a large number of men to defend it, who are generally much better employed in fighting the enemy in the open ; and there is an instinctive feeling that if ever we have to shut up our armies in forts it will be time for us to walk out of India."—GENERAL H. B. MEDLEY, *Royal Engineers.*

" We find that fortification has been sometimes regarded as an end instead of a mere means, that it has been permitted to impose conditions upon strategy and tactics, instead of being made absolutely subservient to both, and that a remedy for defective organization, generalship, training or *moral* has been sought in its employment."—LIEUTENANT-COLONEL SIR G. S. CLARKE, *Royal Engineers.*

IN the first of my *Indian Problems* [1] I showed by facts and figures, which have been ridiculed in-

[1] *Can Russia Invade India ?*

deed, but not refuted, that a Russian invasion of India is an impossibility ; in the second,[1] that that country's present North-West Frontier is strategically and politically unsound ; in the third, I now propose to lay before my readers a statement of the price which India has had to pay for impaired security, and a forecast of the ultimate cost to England of the policy to which she gives a careless and ignorant support.

To arrive at that price, and to estimate that cost, however, many factors which I have hitherto neglected must be taken into account, chief among them being the great defensive works which have been undertaken since Lord Lytton abandoned England's "settled policy" towards Afghanistan, and the military railways within our old frontier, but called into existence by the exigencies of our new one, each of which factors is important enough to require a chapter to itself.

*   *   *   *   *

" Nature," so the late Sir George Chesney told the Aldershot Military Society, " has done a great deal, and nearly closed the frontier, but where there are passes and gorges through the mountains,

[1] *India's Scientific Frontier: Where is it? What is it?*

there field-works have been constructed for the purpose of closing the frontier and strengthening the defences of the important garrison and arsenal of Rawal Pindi, further in the rear."

It would appear from the context that the field-works of which Chesney speaks in this passage were not the long line of fortified posts within our old frontier, which really do close every passage into India, but the forts far in advance of that frontier, in virtue of which we, indeed, occupy the so-called province of Beluchistan, but which are far too weak and isolated to offer any resistance to the advance of a Russian army, such as he must have had in his mind when he attributed to them the office of strengthening the great works of Rawal Pindi. The only fortress outside our old frontier which really blocks a pass leading into India is Quetta, and that, thanks to our mania for road-making,[1] it

[1] "Beside the railway, numerous military roads were constructed north and east of Quetta, and the great Imperial line of communication between Quetta and Dera Ghazi Khan by the Bori Valley, was finally completed and bridged in 1890–91. Considerable progress was also made with another Imperial line, connecting Loralai with the Zhob Valley, and the Zhob Valley with the Gomal Pass and the Punjab ; and

would now be comparatively easy to mask and turn. Against the vast host of invaders, which Sir Charles Macgregor and other illustrious members of the Forward Party saw in their dreams, it would serve no purpose except to give shelter to an Anglo-Indian Army Corps, and keep it safe out of the field ; whilst, viewed in relation to the small force which alone could hope to make its way from the Caspian to the borders of India, its proportions and armament are simply ridiculous ; for what other epithet can be applied to works of which it can be truly said, that " here science has brought to bear every infernal machine in the shape of batteries at short intervals, out-works and breast-works, ranged one behind the other, and quick-firing guns posted on the adjoining heights," [1] whilst all the time, strain one's mental vision as one may, it is impossible to discover any more terrible enemy to be the victim of all

roads were made between the Harnai railway station and Loralai, through the Mahrab Tangi, one of the grandest passes in Beluchistan, and between Harnai and Quetta. Altogether, at the end of 1891, there were in Beluchistan 1,520 miles of road, of which 376 miles were bridged and metalled."—Dr. Thornton's *Life of Sir Robert Sandeman.*

[1] Sir John Dickson-Poynder.

this strength than the hill-tribes, to check whose inroads on our old frontier a score or so of mud forts and a few hundred Native Cavalry used to be found sufficient, since the small Russian force which nature might permit to traverse Afghanistan, is never likely to appear on the scene?

It is Rawal Pindi, however, not Quetta, in which Chesney seems to have discovered the real bulwark of India ; and the fortifications of Rawal Pindi have a curious history, which deserves to be widely known.

Those fortifications, begun in the early days of Lord Lytton's vice-royalty, were originally intended to consist simply of an arsenal, protected by earthworks. When arsenal and earthworks were half completed, some one made the discovery that both were commanded by the adjacent heights ! The site was an impossible one for its purpose, but to confess this by abandoning it, and seeking a better elsewhere, would have brought such disgrace on all the Indian authorities, that Lord Lytton's Government did not dare to face it, and sought to conceal its blunder by turning a modest, useful work into a huge, useless quadrilateral ; which, like Quetta,

would require an army corps for its defence
against a really formidable foe, and whose size
and strength are absurd against any enemy less
than formidable.

And yet, huge as they are, the fortifications
of Rawal Pindi are incomplete, and likely to remain so, since we learn from Sir Henry Brackenbury's contribution to the latest Financial Statement, that, all the necessary forts having now
been erected, "it has been decided to postpone the
construction of the intermediate batteries, as these
could comparatively rapidly be made, and, in view
of the great progress of modern military science, it
is thought that the armament should not yet be
procured." Lack of funds is probably the true
explanation of this patient waiting upon modern
science for the armament of works which Sir
George Chesney pronounced to be "of extraordinary value"; but it is difficult not to suspect,
from the tone of Sir H. Brackenbury's allusion
to the completed forts,[1] that he is as little en-

---

[1] "A series of forts have been completed at Rawal Pindi,
forming a strong entrenched position. These forts required
a long time for construction, and the Government of India
thought it well that they should be made." — See *Indian
Financial Statement for* 1896-97.

amoured of what General H. B. Medley once
styled the "haphazard" fortifications of Rawal
Pindi, as I am.

But, complete or incomplete, armed or un-
armed, the works of Rawal Pindi are only
second in extent and costliness to those of
Quetta, and we are justified in asking—Has the
Indian Government any clear conception of
what it will do with them when a Russian army,
with Fortunatus' cap of invisibility on its head,
his invincible sword in its hand, and, presumably,
his inexhaustible purse in its knapsack, glides
swiftly through the Afghan passes to burst in
unexpected flood upon the plains of India?

Everything in their construction and in the
military treasures they enclose, points to the
permanent character of these gigantic works,
yet Sir George Chesney assured an audience of
British officers, that they were merely "sub-
stitutes" for permanent works, "constructed not
with a view of holding that place in force and
inviting attack there, but simply as a precaution
in the event of our being taken by surprise.
. . . There is a danger," so he went on,
"that we might be caught napping, that war

might find us not ready, and that we might not be in sufficient strength to be able to hold our ground in the open until reinforced by the necessary troops. In that case, we should run considerable risks at the outset, and, therefore, an entrenched position would be of enormous advantage to us as a rallying point before we proceed with the only kind of war which we can ever think of carrying on, that is offensive warfare. These works are of extraordinary value, but it would be a fatal error to suppose the object in their erection was only to hold on to them. If ever we English give up the old policy of offensive war, we may say good-bye to our Indian Empire."

Here we have a man, who for five years had been Military Secretary to the Indian Government, and for yet another five years, Military Member of the Viceroy's Council, confessing that he expected one of the chief factors in our elaborate and costly system of frontier defences to be deserted as soon as it had served as a rallying point for our startled forces. Now, that the smaller fortified posts, scattered over tens of thousands of square miles of mountain and desert, would be abandoned the moment the danger, to guard against which they were constructed, really presented itself, was one of the facts most condemnatory of the Forward School's strategy, which I pointed out in *India's Scientific Frontier*; but I never went so far as to suggest that Rawal Pindi, well within our old boundary, would share the same fate, or that all the vast sums which have been squandered on its fortifications were to buy for us no greater gain than a breathing space in which to make good the criminal ignorance or negligence of the military clique which determines India's foreign and frontier policy.

The prospect is as shameful as it is appalling ; yet I doubt whether it is more to be deprecated than its alternative ; for to cling to the works which have been so casually and mischievously erected, means nothing less than the imprisonment behind their walls of large numbers of troops, whose presence in the field, in the event either of invasion or rebellion, still more in case of the coincidence of the two, would be absolutely essential.   It was the uneasy consciousness of this necessity which drove Chesney into attempting to divest the works, for which he avowed himself largely responsible, of their permanent character.

He was quite right, however, in predicting that if ever the Indian Government gave up taking the offensive in war, we might say good-bye to the British Empire in India, and this, not only because experience has shown that the moral effect of taking the offensive is very great upon Asiatics, but because any other course would cripple us beyond what we could endure. For consider, it is not, as Sir William Mansfield warned us, as if India were England for the purpose of waging war against Russia ; we could not use every soldier, Native or British, within that great peninsula to repel invasion, since the primary object of all our forces in India—but more especially of the British portion of them—is to keep that country for us against the inhabitants of our own provinces, and against the armies of the Native States ; and to relax our hold upon the strategical points which have been selected for this end, including, as they do, arsenals, magazines, treasuries and bridges, would be to court disaster in one direction in seeking to avert it in another ;

and yet, if such fortresses as Rawal Pindi and
Quetta are to be successfully defended, this is
exactly what we shall have to do.   It may
be "monstrous," as Chesney said, "to think
of holding these works for more than temporary
purposes," yet having, like Frankenstein, evoked
our monsters, we shall have to stick to them,
simply because we cannot annihilate them with
a breath, nor yet run the risk of their falling into
foreign or rebel hands; and if we stick to them,
we must either withdraw troops from other military stations, or face our invaders in the open,
with forces so weak as to make defeat almost a
foregone conclusion.   For if we lock up 15,000 or
20,000 men in Quetta, and another 15,000 or
20,000 men in Rawal Pindi, and yet another
15,000 or 20,000 in the works which are to be
hastily improvised at Multan, Lundi Kotal, Jumrud, etc., where is the army for service in the
field to come from, unless we denude other parts
of India of their garrisons?   Let it never be
forgotten that war with Russia in Asia would
mean war with Russia in Europe, and very probably war with France also; and in face of such
a combination, England could spare no reinforce-

ments to India, nor in a period of panic such
as our alarmists picture to themselves, would it
be easy or safe to add largely to our Native army,
or to draw upon the forces of our semi-indepen-
dent allies, at a moment when prudence would
bid us strengthen the camps of observation which
we maintain for the purpose of keeping on those
forces a vigilant eye?

I am arguing, of course, on the Forward
School's assumption that Russia can really invade
India, and in great force, for on no other would
the overgrown fortifications of Rawal Pindi and
Quetta have a word to urge in their own justification; and from that point of view, looking
forward, I behold some future Government of
India impaled upon the horns of a dilemma
prepared for them by Lord Lytton and Lord
Roberts, and by the Secretaries of State, Viceroys
and Military Members of Council, who have
helped to stamp the spirit of those two men—a
spirit strangely compounded of nervous over-
caution and reckless daring—upon India's frontier
policy.

I may be told that my prevision is at fault,
since by the occupation of those 78,000 square

miles of territory, to which I am so wrong-headed as to object, the dilemma in question has been got rid of, as, arrested at our distant outposts, Russian armies would never appear before the walls of Rawal Pindi and Multan, and men enough could be spared from India for the successful defence of Quetta. But why then the fortifications of Rawal Pindi and the promised fortifications of Multan? I am afraid my friends of the Forward Party have as little faith in the efficiency of their latest line of defence as I in its utility, and are as certain that, despite Loralai and Fort Sandeman, Wano and Gilgit and Chitral, yes, despite Quetta itself, those terrible Russians will still fight their way to the Indus, as I am convinced that with Jacobabad and Jumrud, "as the bastions of the front attack," they would never set eyes on that river.

From my point of view—that of the invulnerability of our pre-Lytton frontier—the dilemma can, indeed, never arise ; yet future Indian Governments may reap fruit no less bitter from the policy which has called Rawal Pindi and Quetta into being, and nursed them into the monsters they are to-day, and may lament in vain over the tens of millions of rupees flung into worse than useless permanent—or temporary?—fortifications; millions which, if expended on reproductive works, would have gone far to place England's empire in India on the sure foundations of a contented, because prosperous, people.

From my point of view, also, the evil of Rawal Pindi's haphazard lines begins and ends with themselves; but Quetta has a side more objectionable than the wasteful cost of its fortifications. Its position and the immense military stores collected within its walls call loudly for employment, and there is no lack of restless and ardent spirits among our officers to urge that that call should not be disregarded. Having obtained a base of operations, and the field of operations being in no hurry to come to us, why should not we start out to find it? Quetta, after all, is not the strategically perfect position that 'Forward' politicians once dreamed it was—let us at least turn it to account as a stepping-stone to a better. Kandahar may realize our ideal, or Herat, and, at least, there will be more chance of a fight with the Russians if we move 74, or, still better, 474 miles nearer to their frontier than we are to-day. What matter the dangers that we leave behind us? Is not Quetta there to ward them off, or to keep a refuge for us in case of disaster?

Will any one who knows much of military life say that I have here misrepresented the spirit which pervades a large section of our junior officers, and is not altogether a stranger to their seniors? or can I be accused of vain prophesying when I predict that that spirit, combined with opportunity—and is not Quetta a large and ever-present opportunity?—is pretty sure to land us, sooner or later, not necessarily in war with Russia, because she may wisely keep beyond our reach, but with Afghanistan, that state, inoffensive so far as we are concerned, to which we have twice already done grievous wrong? That spirit is no bad thing in itself; I would not give much for an army if it were not pervaded by love of adventure, by contempt for danger, by the thirst for personal distinction, and the passion for national aggrandizement. But above the military spirit, guiding and restraining it, should stand the higher spirit of the statesman, which, without fearing danger, knows how to discern it; which, ever ready for great exertions, when great exertions are demanded of it, scorns to waste its strength on foolish and futile adventures ; which has risen above the promptings of personal ambition, and has learnt to distinguish wherein the real greatness of a nation consists.

If that wiser, calmer spirit reigned in the councils of the Indian Government, the warlike proclivities of the Anglo-Indian army would be of little consequence ; but unreasoning fear of an impossible contingency has made that Government, for years past, the slave of its military advisers, whose unfitness for the part they have usurped is shown in nothing more conspicuously than in the steady extension of fortifications, designed, by their own confession, *not for the defence of India, but as a refuge for our troops when surprised by a danger*, to discover which, when yet afar off, they have removed their neighbours' landmarks by the score, and have established a long chain of posts of observation, each more isolated and cut off from succour than the one that went before it.

CHAPTER II

MILITARY RAILWAYS

" In India there is little or no publicity, and still less extraneous engineering talent, to criticise the projects emanating from the Public Works Department."—SIR EVELYN BARING (*now* LORD CROMER), *late Financial Member of Viceroy's Council.*

ALTHOUGH the Sind-Pishin branch of the North-Western line is the only railway which has hitherto been constructed on the further side of the Indus with a view to linking Great Britain's new possessions with the Punjab, it would be a gross error to suppose that that branch represents all the misdirected railway effort for which India has to thank her forward school of politicians.

From the category of misdirected effort we must except the completion of the main line of the North-Western Railway, the branch line to Jacobabad, and the protected bridges at Attock and Sukkur,[1] which, in giving to us the power

---

[1] The Attock bridge is 1,655 feet long, and 111 feet above

to operate at will on either side of that great
obstacle the Indus, has put the finishing touch
to the invulnerability of India's natural frontier.
The main line of the North-Western, although
classed, and justly classed, as a commercial
railway,[1] is also a military line in the true sense

the surface of the river at low water, in order to provide
sufficient water-way for the great floods. Its cost was Rs.
3,220,516, but whether with or without its defences is not
clear from the Government records. A strong bridge head
covers the vast structure, and the hills on the right bank of
the river are crowned by forts and heavy batteries. The
bridge at Sukkur is 135 feet shorter than that at Attock, but
its cost—Rs. 3,346,720—was somewhat greater. It, too, is
fitted with block house defences, and covered by outlying
fortifications.

[1] The net earnings of commercial railways on the
standard gauge are, on every train, Rs. 2·09 per mile,
whereas on military lines of the same gauge there is an
admitted loss of Rs. ·4 per train mile ; in other words, every
commercial train that runs 100 miles clears Rs. 209, whilst
every military train is supposed to cost the State, on the
same distance, Rs. 40. In reality the loss is far greater, for
the revenue from military lines, shown in the Administrative
Report, is largely a paper transaction. The gross earnings
of such railways is stated to have been Rs. 3,271,057 in 1895 ;
but this sum, with the exception of a little revenue obtained
from the carriage of salt on the old Lala Musa line, and
some Kafila traffic between Sibi and Rukh, is derived from

of that term, since it unites points of great
strategical importance, whilst doubling their communication with England ; but what shall I say
of the Kushalgarh branch of that railway, or of
the Sind-Sagar line ?

Running through barren and sparsely-peopled
country, whose only mineral product, salt, is
confined to the triangle lying between Attock,
Lala Musa, and Kundian,[1] useless, therefore,
from a commercial point of view, neither of these
lines has paid, or ever will pay, interest on
capital, or even its own working expenses. And
what strategical points do they connect ? Rawal

the transport of troops and stores, and is debited to the
army accounts.

Taking the annual gross earnings of the military railways at Rs. 3,271,057, and the working expenses at Rs.
3,807,375—the figures given in the latest Administrative
Report—and assuming the Rs. 807,375 to be covered by
paying freights, the deficit for every military train which
runs a hundred miles is not Rs. 40, but Rs. 223.

[1] The first 45 miles of the Sind-Sagar Railway being only
intended for the conveyance of salt, were in the first instance
laid down on metre gauge, but when Government determined to convert it into a military line and extend it to
Kundian and Mahmud Kote, they were relaid on a standard
gauge.

Pindi with Kohat ?   Let the unbridged Indus and
empty terminus at Kushalgarh answer that question.[1]   Multan with Lahore ?   That connection
the main line of the North-Western had already
established, and on far surer foundations.   Dera
Ismail Khan and Dera Ghazi Khan with Attock
and Multan ?   A descriptive and historical sketch
of the Sind-Sagar line will enable us to judge
whether this, the end which its authors undoubtedly had in view, has been, or is likely to be,
achieved.

The sanction for the Sind-Sagar Railway was
given in 1884, and the main line—357 miles in
length—seems to have been completed in 1888 ; at
least, I can find no mention in the Indian Financial
Statements of any sums having been allotted for
its construction since that year.   This main line

---

[1] After making this line, which is 79 miles long and
absorbed nine or ten millions (rupees) of public money, the
Indian Government decided against bridging the Indus
at Kushalgarh, on the ground that that point was too near
to the existing bridge at Attock, a discovery which they
surely might have made before beginning it.   A fictitious
air of completeness will shortly be bestowed on this muti-
lated line, by the establishment of a connection between it
and the equally useless Sind-Sagar Railway.

starts from Lala Musa, on the North-Western Railway, twenty-one miles south of Jhelum, and runs for 157 miles due west to Kundian, on the left bank of the Indus. Here it turns to the south and follows the course of the river to Mahmud Kote, whence it takes an easterly direction to Shershah, where it merges again into the North-Western Railway.

Its most remarkable features are the two great bridges, the one over the Jhelum at Chalk Nizam, the other over the Chenab at Shershah.[1] But though, owing to the flatness of the country to be traversed, the Sind-Sagar main line was comparatively easy to make, it is difficult to maintain it in working order on account of the numerous drainage lines which, when the Jhelum, Chenab, and Indus are in flood, spill over and inundate the whole district. Heavy embankments and numerous culverts are supposed to guard it against the encroachments of the water, but, in reality, traffic

[1] Both these bridges greatly exceed that at Attock in length, and the foundations of both have had to be carried down to a depth of 75 ft. below the cold weather level of the rivers they span, on account of the great scour of their waters in flood time.

is often interrupted for days and weeks together. In the rains of 1889, for instance, the Indus rose so persistently that for a long time no repairs could be executed, and the floods, running fourteen miles an hour, endangered all the bridges.

From Kundian the Sind-Sagar Railway is being extended northward 115 miles to Attock, through a singularly wild, barren, and difficult hill country, at an average cost of Rs. 178,750 per mile, the average cost of construction of commercial railways in India being only Rs. 122,659 per mile.

There are no towns along this line, no trade to foster, no agriculture to develop, and its only military use is to bring Attock into communication with Sukkur and Multan, which connection, as I have before mentioned, had already been established on a far securer basis, by the completion of the North-Western Railway, to say nothing of the natural communication by water which had always existed.

In 1891–92, three years after the completion of the Sind-Sagar main line, and after considerable progress had been made with its northern section, the Indian Government took into consideration the question of where and how this railway should be carried across the Indus.

The engineers consulted by it, after pointing out that " the cost of bridging increases as we descend the Indus, by equal increments, from Rs. 2,500,000 at Kushalgarh, to 12,500,000 at Dera Ghazi Khan,"[1] proposed to render the bridging of that river possible at Dera Ismail Khan, by damming up its stream in a gut 3,000 ft. wide ; and if this method of solving the difficulty succeeded in the one case, to execute subsequently similar works at Dera Ghazi Khan. They did not advise any immediate attempt to bridge the gut, which they felt must be tested by several seasons' rains before the stability of its embankments could be counted on ; but to meet the wishes of the military authorities, who were, as they well knew, eager to enter on the construction of railways on the right bank of the Indus, they recommended the immediate establish-ment of steam ferries at Dera Ismail Khan and Dera Ghazi Khan, and the construction of branch lines from the starting-points of these ferries, on the left bank of the river, to Karhi and Ghazi Ghat on the Sind-Sagar line. The engineers con-

[1] *Administrative Report on Railways in India*, 1891-92.

cluded their report by asking for a speedy decision on the main feature of their scheme—the narrowing of the Indus—on the ground that " the works must be executed in a single season, from October to April, or a new survey, with perhaps a new site, might (may) be necessary."

It is difficult to make men who have never seen the Indus, comprehend the insane folly of this project. To confine a stream, often four miles broad, within an artificial gut one-seventh of that width, would be to create a vast lake above the upper end of that channel, and to increase the velocity of its current on issuing from its lower end to so fearful an extent as to ensure the destruction of every "bund" between that point and Sukkur. The Sind-Sagar Railway, if carried to its legitimate conclusion after this fashion, would effectually blot out the Sukkur-Jacobabad section of the Sind-Pishin Railway—probably Jacobabad itself—and sever, once for all, Quetta's precarious communications with India ; and if the monstrous experiment were to be repeated at Dera Ghazi Khan, with the result of creating a second lake between the two guts, there is no foretelling how wide and how far the work of destruction might extend.

Fortunately, the Indian Government was hindered from giving the early decision which had been asked for, by the necessity of consulting the Government of the Punjab before sanctioning a scheme which, by interfering with the irrigation of 30,000 acres of that province, would have unfavourably affected its revenues ; and the delay gave time for the engineers' prognostications to fulfil themselves.

In the course of a year considerable modifications took place in the bed of the Indus, and these combined with "a more complete comprehension of the action of side creeks,"[1] and the necessity of not disturbing valuable cultivation, " necessitated eventually a new scheme for 1892–93," by which a portion, instead of the whole, of the great stream was to be pent-up within the gut and " collateral bridging was to be resorted to."[2] Whether this amended scheme, estimated to cost more than two and a half million rupees, without

---

[1] The Indian Government was fortunate in that a scheme which had been formed in incomplete comprehension of the side-creeks, was not forced through in the winter following on its hasty promulgation.

[2] *Administrative Reports on Railways in India*, 1892–93.

the main bridge, commanded the approval of the
Indian Government, and enters to-day into the
long list of military works which are under official
consideration, I have no means of knowing ; but
the success of the steam ferry lines from the
Sind-Sagar Railway to the Indus, without which
the bridges would have no *raison d'être*, has not
been of a nature to encourage any attempt to
reduce that river to a width " that would be
favourable for bridging," [1] either at Dera Ismail
Khan or at Dera Ghazi Khan.   The line, fourteen miles long, from Karhi to a point on its
left bank opposite the former station, was actually made in 1892, and no sooner had it been
completed, than it was " submerged and seriously
breached before opening for traffic," whilst the
engineers had to confess that the ferry line from
Ghazi Ghat to the main channel of the Indus
was found impracticable, " as the floods rendered
its construction impossible." [2]

From the same report of the Director-General
of Railways, we learn that, " in view of the impracticability of keeping up these branches during

[1] *Administrative Reports on Railways in India*, 1892–93.
[2] *Ibid.*, 1893–94.

the monsoon, it was under consideration whether the Karhi branch (opposite Dera Ismail Khan) should not be dismantled, and the idea of a branch line to Ghazi Ghat abandoned; the material for these branches being, however, kept ready stocked, in case emergency lines should be required."

It appears, therefore, that 565 miles of railway —for the most part utterly useless so far as the material development of the country traversed was concerned—had been constructed, or were in course of construction, by the orders of the Indian Government, in obedience to the counsels of its military advisers, *before any attempt had been made to ascertain whether the purpose it was intended to serve was susceptible of accomplishment*; and that it is kept open, year after year, at a heavy loss to the Indian Exchequer, whilst all the time the Indus forms a safe and permanent line of communication between Attock and the cantonments down stream, and enough steamers and flats to carry a Division could be built for a less sum than is being wasted, month by month, on the Mari-Attock branch of the Sind-Sagar Railway, which will *not* connect Dera Ismail or Dera Ghazi Khan with the great arsenals and military

centres of the Punjab, and which may prove as
open to destructive accidents of all kinds as the
Harnai Valley line, which it will rival in the
number of its viaducts, tunnels, and bridges.

Additional light is being thrown upon the
reckless waste of public money in connection with
this abortive enterprise, by the construction of the
Waziristan-Multan line. This railway will be 157
miles shorter than the Sind-Sagar line, will run
through an irrigable and fertile district, will be
easy and cheap to make, and, judging by its
alignment on the watershed of the Chenab and
the Ravi, it will be above the action of the floods
of either river, and consequently must secure to
Multan a second permanent line of communication with Jhelum and Lahore. But if it will do
this to-day it would have done as much in 1884,
and the Sind-Sagar Railway was as unnecessary
for its secondary, as it has proved futile in regard
to its primary object.

The Sind-Pishin, the Kushalgarh, and the Sind-
Sagar Railways represent all that has hitherto
been accomplished in the matter of military
railways on the North-West Frontier, but many
other lines are projected. As soon as the financial

embarrassments of the Government will permit of the outlay, there is to be a Dera Ismail Khan Railway across the desert to the foot of the Gomal Pass ;[1] a Zhob Valley Railway, to connect the Gomal with the Thal Chotiali route ;[2] a Tochi Railway, to give access to Waziristan ; a Bunnu Railway, to join on to the Tochi line ; and a Peshawur-Michni Railway, to guard the Indian Empire against the danger of a sudden Russian invasion down the Kabul River.

Now, one thing is certain, viz., that if we had remained content with India's frontier as it existed prior to the second Afghan War, not one of these

---

[1] " Including 14 miles of the ferry scheme, this line will be 68½ miles long, and, apart from giving access to the Gomal Pass, it serves *no serious commercial or military object, in a direct sense.*"—*Administrative Report of the Railways in India,* 1892-93.

[2] This line will be 267 miles long, and the estimated cost of the main works amounts to Rs. 48,895,982, one-twelfth or one-thirteenth of the net annual revenue of the whole of India. One 20-mile stretch running along the Gomal River, which will be one succession of tunnels and cuttings, is estimated to cost Rs. 392,000 per mile—more than three times the average cost of the construction of commercial railways in India.—See *Administrative Report of the Railways in India,* 1891-92.

railways would ever have been heard of; the
chain of posts which then watched the mouths
of the Afghan passes being well able to support
each other, or to receive support from larger
stations in their rear, and to hold their own
against any number of mountaineers, shorn of
half their force, and far more than half their
military capacity, by exchanging their hill-sides
for the plains in which our Native troops, especially
our Native Cavalry, are most at home. Soldiers
like the 133 men of the Sind Irregular Horse—all
Hindustanis, be it remembered—who, on the 1st
October, 1847, under the command of Lieutenant
Merewether, first received the charge of a body of
Bugtis, over seven hundred strong, and then, taking
the offensive, literally killed or captured the entire
number, with the exception of two, out of twenty-
five horsemen, who succeeded in making their
escape; soldiers like the 158 men of the 5th
Punjab Cavalry, who, on the 13th March, 1860,
led by Ressaidar Sahadutt Khan, decoyed a force
of three to four thousand Waziris, who had
assembled with the intention of raiding into
British territory, from the shelter of the hills, and
then attacked and totally defeated them, killing

160 men and wounding a large number ; soldiers such as these, I say, with all the advantages of position on their side, had no need of railways to bring up reinforcements from Multan or Lahore, a handful of men from one or two neigh-bouring posts—the posts on our old frontier were only ten to fifteen miles apart—or at worst a couple of regiments from Rajunpur, Dera Ghazi Khan, Dera Ismail Khan, Bunnu or Kohat—were reinforcements enough wherever British territory was threatened.

How different the position to-day! The men may be as brave, but with traitors and spies in their ranks ; shut up among the hills, with no plains at hand into which to draw down their foes and there crush them by a dashing cavalry charge ; with those foes not only in front, but in rear and on either flank, each post too weak to help its neighbour—neighbour in name only, since thirty, even forty miles of difficult country separate one from the other—and with their supports in rear hundreds of miles away, it is no wonder that the Government, responsible for placing troops in so precarious a situation, should strain every nerve to make that situation a little more secure, and, when thwarted in one scheme for providing their new frontier with safe and permanent communications, should fall back upon another, regardless of expense, and without inquiring too narrowly into the practicability of each fresh plan.

" But the Russians ? "

The Russians !

Again and again I have shown that the Russians will never embark on an enterprise in which they cannot hope to be successful ; that India, behind her triple rampart of mountain, desert and river, is, and so long as she forms part of the British Empire, always will be safe from invasion. Now I am prepared to go further, and to maintain that if the Russians *should* determine to attempt the impossible, *should* issue from Afghanistan in unimpaired strength, *should* cross the desert without perishing in thousands of hunger, fever and heat, *should* escape destruction at the hands of our cavalry and horse artillery, India would still have nothing to fear ; for, as the Afghan passes are to the passes of the Balkans or the Alps, so is the Indus, and the country through which it flows, to the Danube or the Rhine and the lands they water.

Rising in the Himalayas, outside British territory, that great river's catch-water basin, before
receiving the waters of the Jhelum, the Chenab,
the Ravi and the Sutlej, is estimated to contain
120,000 square miles—an area equal to that of
Great Britain and Ireland. Above Attock, its
vast volume swelled by its junction with the
Kabul River, it flows for thirty miles in a broad
bed ; below Attock its channel contracts to a
width of from one hundred to four hundred yards,
and its raging, foaming stream runs for ninety
miles between precipitous banks, varying in height
from seventy to seven hundred feet, with a velocity
of from six to ten, or even fourteen miles an hour.
When the snows begin to melt in the high hills,
the pent-up river rises twenty feet above its cold
weather level, and in the monsoon it has been
known to stand seventy feet—on one occasion, in
1841, one hundred feet above that level !

About fifteen miles below Mari the Indus issues
from this ravine and spreads out into an open but
still unfordable stream, five hundred to fifteen
hundred yards wide in winter, and from three to
four miles across in the rains. All along its right
bank, from Dera Ghazi Khan to Sukkur, a net-

work of inundation canals stretch away to the confines of the desert, in itself no insignificant obstacle to the advance of an invading army. These channels, when the river rises, first fill, then disappear beneath its spreading waters, which change a district, hundreds of miles in length and from thirty to forty in breadth, into one vast lake. Where and how could the Russians cross such a river even in the cold weather?—and if they came by the Gomal route, to command which the Sind-Sagar line has been made, it would be in summer, not in winter, that they would arrive on its banks.

Is it to be supposed that they would have carried with them on their long and difficult march, from Kandahar or Ghazni, the pontoons necessary for the bridging of such a stream, even in its quietest and most peaceful aspect? And where on its banks would they obtain the necessary materials, or how, if they could obtain them, would they build their bridge in the teeth of an enemy stronger in numbers and far stronger in position and in resources than they?

These questions I will answer, not in my own words, but in those of Lord Chelmsford, who, in an article on "The Defence of India," published in the *Asiatic Quarterly Review* for July, 1893, wrote as follows :—

"General von Clausewitz, the highest strategical authority of this century, says in his work *On War*: 'As the equipment for crossing rivers which an enemy brings with him, that is, his pontoons, are rarely sufficient for the passage of rivers, much depends on the means to be found on the river itself, its affluents, and in the great towns adjacent ; and lastly, on the timber for building boats and rafts in forests near the river. There are cases in which all these circumstances are so unfavourable that the crossing of a river is by that means almost an impossibility.'

"There are no great towns, there are no great forests within sixty miles of the great Indus river ; and there are only a few insignificant affluents on the right bank. *It would, therefore, be the grossest negligence on the part of the military commanders, if an enemy arriving on the Indus were allowed to secure a single boat available for bridging purposes.*

"Without boats, without timber, with a hostile force on both flanks of the right bank, and a

powerful army on the left bank, ready to oppose
any attempt to cross the river, what chance would
an enemy have of being able to transport from
one bank to the other all the men and material
requisite for such a task as an invasion of India?
If then General von Clausewitz's opinion is to be
accepted, the crossing of the Indus by an enemy,
in such force as to endanger the safety of India,
should be considered not as almost, but as entirely
impossible."

Reason and common sense echo "impossible,"
and, lest their voice should be disregarded, experience comes to their aid. In 1838, for the use of
the Bengal column of the Afghan Expedition, a
bridge was thrown across the Indus from Rohri to
Sukkur, where, in Sind, the river is at its narrowest,
only five hundred yards wide, and where its bed is
divided into two channels by Bukker island ; yet
it took sixteen days, and fifty-five boats, averaging
17 tons in weight, to span the larger of the
two channels between Rohri and the island ; and
four days, and nineteen boats, averaging $7\frac{1}{2}$ tons
in weight, to span the smaller channel between
the island and Sukkur, though there was no
enemy on either bank ; and twice during the

progress of the work the bridge was in danger of
being swept away by floods.[1]

Where those boats once lay moored, a magnifi-
cent iron bridge, covered by a great bridge head,
now carries the North-Western Railway across the
Indus, and an invading army must seek some less
easy spot at which to attempt the passage of that
river ; and where is the spot where it could wait
and work for even twenty days in peace ? There
is none from Attock to Sukkur where we could
not bring an overwhelming force to bear upon its
miserable columns. What justification is there
then for mulcting the Indian people yearly of vast
sums for railways built on the pretence of protecting them against a danger which has no existence,
except in the imagination of timid and ill-informed
politicians, or in the writings and speeches of ambitious military men, who turn the alarm which
they foster to account for the furtherance of
schemes of aggression, not of defence, and who are
not ashamed to base their arguments against the
old North-West Frontier on the assumption of that
" grossest negligence," without which, on the part

---

[1] Major Hough, quoted by Lord Chelmsford.

of the Indian authorities, as Lord Chelmsford
truly says, no enemy can ever cross the Indus.

According to the latest prophet of this faith—
and he only says what all its champions imply—
we are to be deceived, up to the last moment, as to
the route which the Russians will adopt. In this
uncertainty we are to leave the mouth of the
Khyber unprotected and undefended, we are to
have no force at Peshawur strong enough to crush
our enemies should they issue safely from that
defile, nor on the Indus, to render the passage of
that river impossible ; and the roads, rivers, and
railways, which bind all our great military centres
into one great system of defence, are to avail us
nothing ! [1]

The whole of this talk is as ridiculous as it is
disgraceful. If the Indian Government, with its
eyes always fixed on the North-West Frontier,
with hundreds of officers, military and civil, ready
and eager to risk their lives in obtaining for it
trustworthy information, with unlimited funds at
its disposal with which to buy such information
from Native sources, and with all the rumours of

[1] An article in the *United Service Magazine* for October,
1895, by an Officer of the Indian Staff Corps.

:he East reaching it daily by telegraph, *viâ*
Europe, cannot get to know enough of the movements of a vast army on roads hundreds of miles
in length, it is quite unfit to rule a great Empire ;
and if 72,000 British soldiers, and twice that number of Native troops, trained and led by Englishmen, cannot utterly destroy a Russian army,
whenever and wherever it may set foot on Indian
soil, then the Commander-in-Chief in India, and
the heads of all the great departments under his
orders, ought to be incontinently cashiered.

Meantime, will any of my friends of the Forward School be good enough to explain what
miracle is to change ignorance, negligence, and
weakness on the Indus frontier, into knowledge,
vigilance, and strength on that undefined and un-
definable boundary line to which it is impossible
to give so much as a name ?

Statement showing Approximate Cost of the Forward Policy on the North-West Frontier up to 1896,
including the Afghan War of 1878-79-80.

		Rupees.	
I.	The Afghan War	223,110,000 [1]	Sir Evelyn Baring, Financial Member of the Viceroy's Council.
II.	Military Railways on the North-West Frontier since the War	163,967,010 [1]	Administrative Reports on Railways in India.
III.	Beluchistan Agency since the War. Government Allotment, Rs. 365,600 per annum, for sixteen years.	13,849,600	Moral and Material Progress of India, 1893-94, p. 157.
IV.	Special Grants to Beluchistan Agency—		Financial Statements—
	Reservoir in Pishin	Rs. 261,249	1889-90, p. 15, par. 31.
	Quetta Water Works	499,000	1891-92, ,, 23, ,, 16.
	Buildings at Quetta	374,000	1892-93, ,, 32, ,, 64.
V.	Lease of Quetta District, and subsidy in lieu of right to collect tolls in the Bolan Pass since 1883	715,000	Progress and Condition of India, 1891-92, p. 15.
VI.	Preparations for War with Russia in 1885	22,880,710	Official Estimate. Return, dated India Office, 8th June, 1894.
VII.	Special Defence Works on Frontier and Rawal Pindi	30,000,000	Approximate.
VIII.	Military Roads on North-West Frontier; expended principally on the Dera Ghazi Khan and Pishin road	1,000,000 [1]	Financial Statement—1878-80, p. 10.
IX.	Afghan Boundary Commission	1,700,000	Financial Statements—1885-86, p. 22, par. 52. 1894-95, ,, 27, ,, 118.
X.	Permanent Increase of Indian Army in 1885-86—		
	A. 10,753 British Troops	Rs. 95,800,200	
	B. 19,230 Native Troops	65,944,600	Official Estimate. Return, dated, India Office, 8th June, 1894.
	C. Deferred Pay of above British Troops	553,000	
		162,286,600	
XI.	Increase in the Native Pension Establishment, due to the Afghan War, Waziri and Chitral Campaigns, and other Expeditions on North-West Frontier	18,992,700	Approximate.
XII.	Cost to Government of Imperial Service Troops	1,400,000	Progress and Condition of India, 1894-95, p. 169.
XIII.	Re-establishment and Maintenance of British Agency at Gilgit—		
	A. For three years, at the rate of Rs. 50,000 a year	Rs. 150,000	Blue Book, Chitral, p. 26.
	B. ,, loss	500,000	Financial Statements—
	C. Special Grant	90,000	1893-94, p. 7, par. 11.
	D. ,,	481,500	1894-95, ,, 21, ,, 83.
	E. Transport	784,600	1893-94, ,, 7, ,, 11.
	F. ,,	300,000	1893-94, ,, 13, ,, 74.
	G. ,,	100,000	1894-95, ,, 11, ,, 121.
		3,005,900	
XIV.	Re-occupation of the Kuram Valley in 1892-93, at Rs. 450,000 per annum, for three years	1,350,000	Financial Statement—1893-94, p. 7, par. 11.
XV.	Grants for so-called Mobilisation—		Financial Statements—
	A. 1889	Rs. 2,035,000	1889-90, p. 24, par. 57.
	B. 1890	660,000	1890-91, ,, 6, ,, 12.
	C. 1891	2,134,000	1892-93, ,, 8, ,, 13.
	D. 1892	656,000	
		5,385,000	
XVI.	Additional Transport Animals, Re-mounts, and Mules—		Financial Statements—
	A. 1891	Rs. 1,321,000	1892-93, p. 8, par. 13.
	B. 1893	269,000	1894-95, ,, 6, ,, 9.
	C. 1894	237,000	1894-95, ,, 8, ,, 121.
		1,825,000 [1]	
XVII.	Rise in price of food, forage, and increase of number of animals to be fed—		Financial Statements—
	A. 1889	Rs. 795,000	1889-90, p. 24, par. 57.
	B. 1892	1,500,000	1893-94, ,, 7, ,, 11.
	C. 1893	700,000	1893-94, ,, 27, ,, 83.
	D. 1894	490,000	1894-95, ,, 6, ,, 121.
		3,485,000	
XVIII.	Expeditions on North-West Frontier since 1888-89	3,073,680	Official Estimate. Return, dated, India Office, 8th June, 1894.
XIX.	Minor operations (not scheduled) since 1884-85	3,239,100	Official Estimate.
XX.	Waziri Campaign, including cost of Delimitation Commission, Fortified Post and Tochi Cantonments	3,824,000	Financial Statements— 1893-96, p. 15, par. 56, and p. 56, par. 700. 1896-97, ,, 34, ,, 132.
XXI.	Chitral Campaign, including occupation of Chitral during past and present year	21,500,000	Financial Statement—1896-97, p. 7, par. 11, and footnote.
XXII.	Khyber Rifles raised after the War	1,398,240	Progress and Condition of India, 1891-92, p. 17.
XXIII.	Subsidies—		
	A. Amir of Afghanistan since the War	Rs. 21,000,000	13 years at 12 lakhs, 3 at 18 lakhs.
	B. Khyberes	1,400,620	Progress and Condition of India, 1891-92, p. 17.
	C. Ruler of Chitral and his brothers	60,000	Chitral Blue Book, pp. 9 and 13.
	D. Gomal Chiefs since 1890	296,760	Progress and Condition of India, 1891-92, p. 17.
	E. Other small Chiefs on North-West Frontier	100,000	,, ,, ,, ,, pp. 16 & 18.
		22,857,200	
	Total Rupees	**714,580,060**	

[1] Plus railways earning were cannot and by the English Exchequer in the War Expenses.
[1] Provision is made in the Budget Estimate for 1896-97, for a further sum of Rs. 2,411,000 to be expended on these military railways.
[1] A large sum has been spent on defensive and military establishments at Quetta, including an advanced position covering the place, storage, roads and culverts for various bridges, tunnels, etc. on the Sind-Pishin Railway. An estimated amount has been formed at Rawal Pindi, and a defensive post at Mardan.—Indian Finance Statement for 1896-97.
[1] This sum only represents a small portion of the money expended on military roads in Beluchistan and other places beyond the Indus, as large sums are annually disbursed by both the military and civil departments in building new roads and maintaining the old ones.
[1] Provision is made in the Budget Estimate for 1896-97, for Rs. 1,940,000 for preparations for mobilisation of the Field Army.
[1] The maintenance of the Transport Branch of the Commissariat Department costs, in 1893-94, no less than Rs. 3,968,000; but, in the following year, a larger sum where called upon to provide carriage for the Chitral or 15,000 men mobilised for the relief of Chitral.

Comparative Statements of Home Remittances and Expenditure on Army, Police, and Political Department, exclusive of exchange except in first item, between the Financial years 1877-78 (the year preceding the Afghan War) and 1895-96.

	Accounts, 1877-78.	Revised Estimate, 1895-96.	Increase.	Remarks.
	Rupees.	Rupees.	Rupees.	
Secretary of State's Bills sold	116,985,000	320,982,000	203,997,000	An increase of four-fifths.
Army	£10,134,000 or 166,797,610	£18,300,000 or 284,133,000 [1,2]	£8,166,000 57,735,390	An increase of more than a third.
Police	21,582,370	40,091,000	18,508,630	An increase of nearly double.
Political Department	4,689,750	10,199,000	5,509,250	An increase of more than double.

[1] Exclusive of Military Works, Special Works, and Deferred Pay, on all of which items there has been a considerable increase.
[1] In 1877-78, the year preceding the Afghan War, the commutation charges were Rs. 22,590,000; in 1895-96 they had risen to the great sum of Rs. 36,240,500.—See Return, dated, India Office, 8th June, 1894.

CHAPTER III

COST OF THE FORWARD POLICY

" The true cause of India's financial perplexities is the restless frontier policy that has been pursued for the last ten years, side by side with the reckless outlay on railways." —A. K. CONNELL, M.A.

" The facts which I have brought to your notice may be briefly recapitulated — an Eastern country governed in accordance with expensive Western ideas, *an immense and poor population*, a narrow margin of possible additional revenue, a constant tendency for expenditure to outgrow revenue, *a system of Government in India favourable to increase of, and unfavourable to reduction of, expenditure, no financial control by intelligent and well-informed public opinion either in India or in England*, an insufficient check on expenditure in India, a remote and imperfect control exercised from England, a revenue specially liable to fluctuations year to year, and growing foreign payments."—SIR DAVID BARBOUR, *Late Financial Member Viceroy's Council.*

" In every one of the eight years after 1885 net Indian military expenditure increased on the average by more than the whole increase during the ten years before 1885."—SIR W. WEDDERBURN, M.P.

" If we enter on a course of successive measures of fresh taxation, Russia, without moving a man or a gun, need only to bide her time. If slow and sure is her game, surely and slowly we shall be playing her hand for her."—SIR AUCKLAND COLVIN, *Late Financial Member Viceroy's Council.*

THE accompanying table contains the official confession of the cost of the Forward Policy to the people of India, a confession that is very far from telling the whole tale of cruel exactions and dangerous waste which is the true history of that policy.

Take, for instance, the first item in that table, the cost of the Afghan War—Rs. 223,110,000—and see how it expands in the light of Major Evelyn Baring's admission, in his Financial Statement of the year 1882–83, that "it cannot be doubted that a great deal of the expenditure debited to the ordinary (military) account really belongs to the war," and that money spent "by reason of it"—the war—"was set down among civil charges." In proof of this latter assertion he adduced the fact that the Punjab Northern State Railway, the construction of which had to be hurried on for the purpose of moving up troops and supplies, cost, on that account, considerably more than it otherwise would have done, and yet not a rupee of this enhanced price was debited to war expenditure;[1] but he made no mention of the large sums spent, during the three years the war lasted, by the political officers in buying the services or the neutrality of the tribesmen, either

[1] *Indian Financial Statement for* 1882–83.

individually or collectively, along the three lines of advance, nor yet of the cost of those political officers themselves, taken from their Indian appointments, yet still drawing their pay from the Civil List, though both these forms of expenditure were due to the war.

There is nothing to surprise us in these deceptive classifications; they are the natural outcome of the desire to minimise the cost of a policy which runs counter to the wishes and interests of the people who have to pay for it ; and they are as common as they are natural, vitiating the official figures for all the frontier expeditions and minor operations, just as much as they falsify those of the Afghan War. One proof of this, but that a very glaring one, must suffice.

During a period of ten years—from 1885 to 1895—great activity prevailed all along our frontier, from Quetta to Gilgit, from Sikkim to Burma, the expeditions and operations on its north-west section alone admittedly absorbing Rs. 52,569,500. In reality they cost considerably more.

In the Financial Statement for the year 1888–89, Rs. 2,035,000 were set down to mobili-

zation—an entirely new item of expenditure—
which was thus explained and defended by
Sir David Barbour, then the Financial Member
of Council : "The Rs. 2,035,000 on account of
mobilization is intended to meet the cost of
purchasing transport animals, provisions, and
equipment, so that, in case of need, an army
corps may be in a position to take the field
promptly.   This is one of those precautions which,
in the present day of scientific warfare, cannot be
neglected.   *The greater portion of the cost will
be incurred once and for all, and will not recur.*" [1]
The   Rs. 2,035,000   proved   insufficient   for   the
purpose in view, and the Financial Statement
for 1890–91 contained a further provision of
Rs. 600,000, "to complete the arrangements and
preparations to facilitate mobilization."

To people of my views, the need of providing
for the mobilization of an army corps, *for service
across the frontier*, was not apparent ; but we derived a certain amount of comfort from the assurance that the process, unnecessary as we thought
it, and expensive as it certainly was, had been
completed, and we noted with satisfaction the

[1] *Indian Financial Statement*, 1889–90, page 24, par. 57.

absence of the word *mobilization* from the Financial Statement for the year 1891–92. All the greater, therefore, were our disappointment and astonishment when, in the course of the same year, a revised estimate was made public, in which, besides Rs. 800,000 "sanctioned during the year for additional transport mules," and Rs. 521,000 "for remounts and ordnance mules," [1] Rs. 2,134,000 were set down as "*Expenditure in India in preparations to facilitate mobilization*"; whilst the Financial Statement for 1892–93 placed Rs. 616,000 to the account of "*Measures intended to facilitate the speedy mobilization of the army.*"

Now, if Rs. 2,635,000 was an adequate provision for the mobilization of an army corps—there was never any talk of mobilizing two—what became of the transport, provisions, and equipment bought with that money? There can be but one answer to the question—it had all disappeared, used up in frontier expeditions and minor operations; and, so far as transport is concerned, we have the clearest proof that the Rs. 2,750,000 nominally devoted to mobilization in 1891–92

---

[1] See Table of Costs, XVI. A, 1891, Rs. 1,321,000 (Rs. 800,000 + 521,000).

and 1892-93 went the same way, for when in
the spring of 1895 a single division—minus the
greater part of its cavalry and its horse and field
artillery—was ordered on active service, it was
found that there were only 7,482 Government
mules available, and the military authorities, after
buying or hiring every baggage animal that they
could lay hands on, were reduced to the necessity
of borrowing the transport service of the Jaipur
and Gwalior Imperial Service Troops, and de-
priving a number of our own regiments of their
regimental baggage ponies.[1]

In the current year Rs. 4,949,000 have again
been devoted to the mobilization of a field army,

---

[1] Sir Henry Brackenbury, Military Member of the
Viceroy's Council, in his remarks on the military expenditure in 1895-96, mentions that "no less than 40,000 transport animals were employed with the Chitral Relief Force."
As regards camels, he said : " We were dependent entirely
upon hired camels, or upon camels purchased expressly for
the campaign. . . . But the number which could be
hired was extremely small, and at the very outset the
Government was obliged to have recourse to purchase. . . .
*The camels purchased by Government have for the most
part so broken down in health that it has been found impracticable to retain any but a very small number of them
for future use.*"

and Sir James Westland has promised the Indian taxpayer that Rs. 4,348,000 of that amount "*will be non-recurring, initial expenditure.*" Can he, I wonder, ever have read his predecessor's similar assurance ? The sum is large, nevertheless it is absolutely certain that if, in the course of the next two or three years, India should become involved in "scientific warfare," she would find herself utterly destitute of the means of prosecuting it, unless indeed her Government had meanwhile put a stop to the expeditions and operations which are perpetually frittering away her resources of all kinds, but more especially her supply of transport cattle.

It is worth noting that this habit of concealing the true cost of past expeditions and operations is closely allied to that tendency to under-estimate the probable expense of each new phase of the expansion fever, to which we owe the most stupendous financial blunder on record—the es-timating of the total net cost of the Afghan War at £5,752,000 in February, 1880, and the revision of that estimate in June of the same year by rather more than £9,000,000 ! The £15,000,000 at which the cost of the war was then placed, rose in October to £15,777,000, and when the accounts were made up at the close of the financial year—March, 1881—this sum was found to have fallen short of the monies already expended by £828,000, whilst war expenditure still showed no sign of coming to an end![1]

The story is so old a one that there has been time for most of us to forget it, but we all know that it has repeated itself in still more startling form, though on a smaller scale, à propos of that campaign which so unpleasantly laid bare the deficiencies of Indian transport arrangements, and the untrustworthiness of Indian Budgets.

The first estimate for the Chitral Expedition amounted only to Rs. 1,500,000 ; the sum actually spent upon it, to Rs. 17,647,000, or nearly twelve times more than that estimate ; whilst, according to Sir James Westland, "it has left us a legacy of permanent expenditure in the occupation of Chitral and of its communications, which has involved in 1895–96 an expenditure of Rs. 1,022,000, and will involve in 1896–97

[1] *Indian Financial Statement for* 1881-82.

an expenditure of Rs. 2,317,000 . . . irrespective of the Political Expenditure which comes to Rs. 200,000 in 1895–96, and Rs. 220,000 in 1896–97 ; . . . also of Military Works Expenditure, Rs. 216,000 in 1896–97."[1]

The Indian Finance Minister adds that "it is expected that it will be possible to reduce these figures when we pass beyond the initial stages of the occupation," but the expectation derives no support from our experience in Gilgit, where the cost of occupation quadrupled in the third year—1891–92—and has never since declined.[2]

I shall probably be reminded that Sir J. Westland explained away the discrepancy, I have noted, by the remark that "the Budget provision of Rs. 1,500,000 was intended to meet the cost of preparations which it was hoped might not eventuate in war"; to which I answer that such hopes had as little foundation as the expectations mentioned above, and that they reflect great discredit on the knowledge and judgment of those entertaining them, for

[1] *Indian Financial Statement for* 1896–97.
[2] *Chitral Blue Book*, page 20.

surely, if there be one thing more than another
which our frontier experience ought to have
taught the Indian Government, it is that the
mountain tribes of the north and north-west
never submit tamely to the passage of British
troops through their territories, however reas-
suring the proclamation which heralds their
approach, nor to the construction of roads, in
which *we* may see instruments for the preservation
of their independence from Russian aggression, but
they can recognise nothing but the time-honoured
means by which that independence is confiscated by ourselves.

As I am on the subject of Chitral, I will
note here one of the many deceptions practised,
consciously or unconsciously, on the British
public by the English official defenders of the
Forward Policy.   It will be remembered that
Mr. Balfour, in a speech made at Manchester
last autumn, assured his audience that there had
been no augmentation of the Anglo-Indian
army as a consequence of the occupation of
Chitral.   Now, it is true that no troops have
been *openly* added to that army, either before,
or after the Chitral campaign ; nevertheless,

there was an increase of 1,861 British and 1,565 Native troops in 1893-94, the year in which the Indian Government succeeded in extorting from the Amir of Afghanistan his consent to the establishment of British influence over the Independent Tribes ; in 1894-95, on the eve of the Chitral expedition, an increase of 1,726, in the autumn of last year, of 946, and at the beginning of this year, of 1,508 British troops, bringing up the total strength of the British forces in India to 78,043 officers and men, 6,041 in excess of the sanctioned establishment,[1] and adding thereby five and a quarter million rupees to India's annual military burdens. These successive augmentations of the Indian army—augmentations entirely unauthorized, so far as I can discover—can have had but one cause and excuse, viz., the necessity of providing for that further development of the Forward Policy for which Sir Mortimer Durand's negotiations at Kabul paved the way. The occupation of Chitral has been part of that development, and Mr. Balfour's statement was, therefore, nothing better than a misleading

[1] See Note [1] next page.

quibble, though he himself was probably one of
the misled.

To return from this digression.

My table represents then, in very inadequate
fashion, the *direct* cost of the Forward Policy

[1] Establishment before increase in the Army was sanctioned in 1885–86.	British Troops	61,158
	Native Troops	129,483
	Total ...	190,641
Establishment after sanctioned increase. (Return East Indian [Army], dated September 16th, 1887, page 187.)	British Troops	72,002
	Native Troops	148,498
	Total ...	220,500
Strength of the Army, April 1st, 1894. (See: *Moral and Material Progress in India for* 1893-94, page 171.)	British Troops	73,863
	Native Troops	150,063
	Total ...	223,926

Average strength of the British Troops in 1895 ...   75,589
(General Annual Return of British Troops, 1895.)
Strength of Native Troops, April 1st, 1895   ...   149,963
(*Moral and Material Progress in India*, 1894-95,
   page 128.)

                                    Total   ... 225,552

Strength of British Troops in India on the 1st
   January, 1896, including 1,508 men on their way
   out to that country   78,043
(General Annual Return of the British Army for
   the year 1895.)

to the Indian people ; it throws no light on the *indirect* price which they have had to pay for it, great as that price has been. When we consider the enormous amount of labour which, during the last eighteen years, has been turned, more or less by force, into unproductive channels, and the vast number of lives sacrificed, whether in the making of military roads and railways, or in the transport of stores of all kinds to distant outposts ; when we add to this drain upon India's first element of prosperity—her industrious population—the waste of her resources in the shape of beasts of burden—camels, mules, ponies, donkeys, and bullocks—withdrawn for the same purposes from the service of the peasant, in districts where not only the actual cultivation of the soil, but often the very possibility of such cultivation depends upon their use, and from the service of the trader, in regions where trade has no other means of transit—we stand aghast at this silent bleeding to death of a people whom most Englishmen honestly desire to benefit. Of the waste of human and animal life in the two Afghan Wars—the latter duly chronicled in official reports, the former passed over in

discreet, or indifferent silence—I have spoken
in a former volume, and I will not recur to it
here, but rather try to impress upon my readers
the sad truth that that waste is still going on,
and will not cease so long as military roads
and railways continue to be made, and so long
as thousands of troops have to draw their supplies from a distant base, over rough mountain
roads, toiling along which the men and beasts
of the hot plains are often exposed to bitter
frost and deadly icy winds.

There is a passage in the *Administrative Report
of Indian Railways for the year* 1886–87, which
throws a lurid light upon the former of these two
great sources of human suffering and death :—
" The heat (on the Harnai Valley line) from
May to August, 1886, was terrific, and so trying
on many occasions, it seemed impossible to go on
with the work. The staff suffered terribly from
fever ; *the plate-laying gangs were practically
renewed every month by fresh importations from
India* as they melted away from fever, dysentery,
and scurvy. In the same way the gangs of girder
erectors dropped off, and *during four months were
twice replaced from India.*"

The picture, in its official conciseness, is grim enough, but its colours darken when we remember that all these lives were thrown away on a work which, within five years, was condemned as unsafe and untrustworthy,[1] on which, nevertheless, we are still relying for keeping open communications with Quetta, because the line that was to supersede it, constructed under the same conditions and assuredly at the same cost to its makers, is still unopened to traffic, though its completion was promised first for last summer, and then for the end of last year;[2] nor is the gloom of that picture relieved by the reflection that the Harnai Railway and all other military lines are perpetually being

[1] "This railway has been constructed at great expense— 20 million rupees—but unfortunately it has been found, after working about five years, that its foundations are unsound, and at certain stages of the line they are nothing better than dry mud, which, during the rains, is converted into pulp, with the inevitable result that whole portions of the line fell away, making it totally useless. *As this railway was constructed for purely strategical purposes in case of war, it must be said to have failed in its purpose.*"—SIR JOHN DICKSON-POYNDER, Bart., M.P.

[2] "It has a gradient which in places is as steep as any in the world, and enormous motive power will be required to drag up a heavy train."—SIR JOHN DICKSON-POYNDER.

reconstructed, so that the toll of death which they exact is never fully paid.

No military road has a darker tale to tell than the old road to Gilgit, since, in 1876, the Maharajah of Kashmir, at the instigation, or command of Lord Lytton, made that fort a base from which to obtain control over Chitral and Yassin. The hateful *Be-gar*—forced labour—on this dreaded road has torn the peasant from his plough, the craftsman from his hammer or his loom, yes, even the merchant from his shop. To escape that deadly slavery, hundreds of families have fled from their homes, leaving their villages to fall to ruins, and their fields to return to the waste.

To mitigate this drain upon the human wealth of the country, an English contractor was called in, who undertook to construct a new road, ten feet wide, with a gradient of 1 in 10, by the first of July, 1893 ; but in the early summer of that year the work was found to have been greatly damaged by floods, and again hundreds of miserable coolies, and their equally miserable beasts, had to carry the food and military stores, the very forage of a growing garrison, up the narrow, slippery, windswept path, on which so many of their brothers had previously perished. Whether, or not, that new road has ever come into use, I have been unable to ascertain,[1] but I do know that so far from being completed at the date specified, Rs. 450,000 were spent upon it by Kashmir in 1893-94, and that, when the Pamir Delimitation Commissioners went up to Gilgit last year, it was not by it that they travelled ; and I can safely predict that in every exceptional season—and most seasons are exceptional in those regions—the three or four months during which it may be free from snow will be taken up in repairing it, and traffic will have to revert to its old track.[2]

But supposing the new road to be completed and to be kept in good working order, and suppos-

[1] Apparently the Indian Government is not anxious that any information should leak out, for according to a private letter from Kashmir this summer, "at present the ordinary traveller is only allowed to go as far as Gurais, three marches from Bandipur, at the head of the Wulur Lake, and the route to Gilgit is only open to the Gilgit garrison."

[2] Difficult and dangerous as the old Gilgit road may be, it, doubtless, follows the line which long experience has proved to be the least exposed to the destructive agencies of nature. Icy blasts and snowstorms may kill the traveller, but floods and landslips leave him no path by which to travel.

ing a transport corps to be organized for the yearly victualling of Gilgit, that corps must consist of men and mules taken from useful occupations, and Kashmir would still have to lose their productive labour, and to pay for their maintenance in worse than idleness, since the more mouths the Indian military authorities can contrive to feed beyond the Indus frontier, the louder will they clamour for more troops wherewith to strengthen old garrisons, or to establish new ones, and the heavier will grow the burdens that the Kashmiri and Indian peoples have alike to bear.[1]

Those burdens may seem light to us who, with a seventh of the population of India, raise more than double her revenue, but to her, in her deep poverty, they are simply crushing. Poverty is the cardinal fact of the situation which, in three suc-

[1] The annual revenue of Kashmir amounts to little more than Rs. 5,000,000 ; her military expenditure, roughly speaking, to Rs. 3,500,000. For the maintenance of the Imperial Service Corps alone she is paying Rs. 1,000,000 a year. Small wonder, then, that the compiler of the *Progress of India for the year* 1894-95, had to record a deficit of 11½ lakhs in the Kashmir State accounts for 1893-94, the year's revenue amounting to Rs. 5,073,870 and the expenditure to Rs. 6,242,750.

cessive volumes, dealing with its different aspects, I have been trying to make clear to my readers, and yet the fact most difficult to bring home to their minds. To most Englishmen the very name, India, conjures up visions of wealth and splendour, of luxurious courts at one end of the social scale, and silver-bangled peasants at the other. The luxurious courts still flourish, but the silver-bangled peasantry are on the decline, bracelets of lac and brass taking the place of bracelets of the precious metal. No people in the world are more heavily taxed, in proportion to their means, than the Indian people under British rule, none live more constantly on the brink of starvation.[1] We hear

[1] "The burden of life in British India has become heavier, and is much harder to bear. Assessments in some cases are four times higher than they were wont to be ; salt is much more heavily taxed, rights over grazing lands have been abolished, fuel is harder to get, with the result that the labouring classes can barely provide sustenance for themselves and their families even in the most hand-to-mouth fashion."—W. DIGBY, C.I.E.

"I do not hesitate to say that half our agricultural population never know from year's end to year's end what it is to have their hunger fully satisfied."—SIR CHARLES ELLIOTT, *Late Member of the Viceroy's Council, and Lieutenant-Governor of Bengal.*

much of the paternal Government which watches over its vast family, ever ready to hasten to the aid of its distressed children ; but there is little paternal in a government which first spreads universal destitution and then relieves it in isolated cases, too often mitigating famine in one district by creating scarcity in another.

I could give endless proofs of the depth and extent of the poverty which prevails in India, but a few will suffice.

Salt is a necessity of life, yet when the tax upon salt was increased 25 per cent. in 1889, the consumption of that necessity fell, with a growing population, from 34,330,000 to 31,474,000 maunds ;[1] and whilst in Burma, where the duty is only one rupee per maund, the consumption of salt is 17 lbs. per head, it is only 10½ lbs. in Bengal, and 8 lbs. per head in the North-West Provinces and Oudh. Is it conceivable that any cause short of utter inability to buy more would induce the Indian *ryot* to stint himself in a commodity which is essential to his health and to the health of his cattle, and without which all food is tasteless and un-inviting ?

[1] *Progress and Condition of India for* 1894-95.

The 3½ per cent. duty on imported cotton goods, obnoxious to the Lancashire manufacturer, produced in the financial year 1895–96 Rs. 11,685,000, about one-third of an anna, or less than a halfpenny, per head of the entire population of India, including the inhabitants of the Native States ; the excise yields nearly 57 million rupees per annum, or about three annas, barely 2½d., per annum per head of the population directly ruled by the English, taking the rupee at 14d. ; and the greater part of this sum is paid " by the Europeans in India themselves, by their native underlings, together with the few rich natives who have contracted European habits."[1]

Does any one suppose that intoxicating drinks and opium have no attraction for the Indian lower classes, or that they have a conscientious objection to English calicoes and prints, or, indeed, to clothing of any description, because a loin-cloth for outdoor and a cotton coat for indoor wear is all the covering that many men possess?

The tax or rent owed by all owners of land to Government may be taken roughly at only one rupee per head of the population, yet it is too often

[1] *Investors' Review*, September, 1895.

paid with the greatest difficulty, and in many cases cannot be paid at all ; so that suits for recovery of rent and arrears are common all over India, and most rigorously enforced.   The lightness of this tribute, coupled with the difficulty often experienced in collecting it, is the best proof of the indigence of the Indian people, and of the critical condition of the Indian Government, which, straining in ordinary times the taxpaying capacity of its dominions to the breaking point, has no resource in reserve on which to fall back in seasons of emergency.   That Government sucks the life-blood of its subjects to no purpose, and grows the poorer for every million wrung from their necessities, for the Forward Policy's insatiable maw swallows up each increase in revenue as it accrues.

In 1888–89, *the year of the re-occupation of Gilgit*, it not only added that 25 per cent. to the hated and inhuman salt tax, the effect of which I have already mentioned—it laid hands on a portion of the balances of the Provincial Governments, and confiscated the fund consecrated to the prevention of famine.   In 1894–95, *a year which bore the firstfruits of Sir Mortimer Du-*

rand's agreement with Abdur Rahman, in the Waziri War and the initial preparations for the Chitral Expedition; and again in 1895-96, when that expedition was carried out—both these acts of spoliation were repeated ; and, if in the current year the famine fund is to be partially re-established,[1] and the balances of the Provincial Governments restored, these acts of restitution are due to a variety of fortuitous circumstances, chief among them a rise in the value of the rupee, a rise which a dozen different causes may at any moment transform into a fresh fall.[2]

The later Indian Financial Statements teem with confessions and regrets.

" The reduction under Construction of Railways is due to the fact that we have no surplus revenue to devote to such purposes " (F.S., 1893-94). " The decrease of Rs. 3,707,000 under Buildings and Roads is due to economies forced upon us by our present financial condition. We have saved

---

[1] The Government of India decided on a partial reduction of the Famine Relief Fund on the eve of a famine which promises to equal, if not exceed, that of 1876-78, in which the mortality was appalling, and which entailed an expenditure of £18,550,336.

[2] *Indian Financial Statement for* 1896-97.

Rs. 1,942,000 by reducing the grant for Military Works, and Rs. 1,760,000 by cutting out practically every new work upon the Civil side . . . to which we are not absolutely committed " (F. S., 1894-95, p. 8). "The next measure is that we are obliged to suspend the famine grant for the time.   This is, as has often been explained, the grant of surplus revenue to the construction of Protective Railways and Irrigation Works. . . . The principal railway work which is being charged to this head at present is the East Coast Railway. As this work is classed also as a productive work, a considerable grant has been given to it under the head of expenditure not charged against revenue, so that this particular work will not very greatly suffer by the suspension of the grant. But this only means that the effect of the reduction is passed on to other railway projects.

"One other measure we have been obliged to take, namely to call on Provincial Governments for contributions to our aid ; in other words, *to force upon them severe economies, and appropriate the result to the benefit of our own account.* The Government of India were most unwilling to have recourse to a measure *which practically means the*

*stoppage for the time of all administrative improve-
ment—a measure which they feel must take all
the heart out of Provincial Governments by making
them surrender all the fruits of careful administration to fill the yawning gulf of our sterling
payments"* (*Ibid.*, pp. 9, 10).

"We have no surplus to devote to the construction of Protective Railways, and the Famine
Insurance grant must for the present remain in
partial abeyance" (F. S., 1895-96).

"Although every economy has been enforced,
the Provincial balance has been reduced to a
figure which, especially in view of the scarcity
impending in some parts of the (N.W.) Province,
cannot be regarded as safe" (F. S., 1896-97).

How well the admission that the confiscation
of the Provincial balances meant "practically the
stoppage, for the time, of all administrative improvement," accords with Lord Mansfield's warning that the occupation of Afghanistan (the name
being used by him in its broadest sense) would
prove the stoppage of progress in India !

But am I justified in attributing the financial
difficulties of the Indian Government to its Forward Policy ?   Does not one of the passages,

which I myself have quoted, claim for them
another source, viz., the great change that has
taken place in the relative value of gold and
silver? It is not "the yawning gulf" of military
expenditure, but of "sterling payments" which
the Financial Member of Council accuses of compelling him to rob the Provincial Governments of
"all the fruits of their careful administration."

I am aware that the Exchange difficulty first
made itself severely felt in 1885–86; yet this
knowledge cannot shake my conviction that the
financial embarrassments of the Indian Government
are due far more to the Forward Policy on the
North-West Frontier than to the depreciation of
the rupee. It is quite true that the loss from the
latter cause since that year has reached the enormous sum of Rs. 870,972,240, whilst the former, on
the North-West Frontier, has cost India, directly,
only Rs. 714,580,480; but no one, I suppose, will
dispute that two burdens weigh more heavily than
one, and that, if the Indian Government had not
had to provide the smaller sum, the expenditure
of which was optional, it would have been in a
better position to provide the larger sum, if such
provision had still been incumbent on it. But the

Forward Policy has largely swelled the Home Charges, on which the depreciation of the rupee is felt by the Indian Government, how largely the reader will understand when he learns that, if those charges had remained unchanged from what they were prior to the Afghan War, India would have saved in exchange, in the year 1895–96 alone, no less than 146½ millions of rupees.[1]

And if there had been no triumph of the Forward Policy in 1878, and no renewal of its ascendency in 1885, and India had been spared the Afghan War and all the expense of subsequent expeditions and occupations ; and if of the Rs. 714,580,480 which these enterprises absorbed, one-half had remained in the pockets of the Indian people, and the other half had been spent on irrigation works and on commercial railways and roads—especially on feeder lines and roads to bind village to village and town with country, from one end of India to the other—can any one believe that the depreciated rupee would have endangered the solvency of her Government?

The following table, which I borrow from Mr.

[1] See Comparative Statement at foot of Table.

MacGeorge's valuable volume, *Ways and Works in India*, throws a flood of light on the results of such wise expenditure, a light in which the exchange difficulty melts into insignificance, for my hypothetical irrigation works, major and minor alike, would have been constructed out of revenue, not with borrowed capital, and the whole profits of the investment would have gone to Government.

Irrigation and navigation work return for all India, 1890–91, except Sind and North-West Provinces, which are for 1889–90. Given in sterling, not rupees :—

Main Canal and Branches.	Of which are Navigable.	Distributing Channels.	Area Irrigated, 1890–91.
Miles.	Miles.	Miles.	Acres.
16,026	2,882½	23,696¾	13,353,069, or 20,864 square miles

Value of Irrigated Crops, 1890–91.	Capital Outlay up to end of 1890–91.	For Year 1890–91.	
		Net Revenue earned.	Per cent. on Capital.
£ 23,879,607	£ 32,040,290	£ 1,829,741	£ 5·74

Note.—Value of irrigated crops for 1890–91 was equal to nearly three-quarters of the whole capital outlay. See columns 5 and 6.

This table shows what the cultivator pays for the water supplied to him, but not the great gain which, at the next Land Settlement, will be reaped by the Government in the shape of a largely enhanced land revenue, the rental of irrigated land in Northern India being two to three times that of unirrigated, and in Madras up to twelve and fifteen times as much.

No; whatever it may allege in the apologies which, from time to time, it is driven to put forward, the Indian Government must be well aware that the fall in exchange, though it has done something to increase its difficulties, is not their cause; and it cannot doubt that, with a prosperous people and an expanding revenue, it would never have been reduced to shifts which it practises with anxiety, and confesses with shame.

For the shame I have shown good cause. I have still to prove that the anxiety is equally legitimate.

The poverty which I have described breeds discontent, and the discontent calls loudly for an increase in the only power on which India's alien rulers can rely for the suppression of disturbances and insurrectionary movements.

Yet, notwithstanding an addition of 37,365 men to the Anglo-Indian army, the Indian Government's military position within its own provinces is weaker than it was, and tends to become weaker still. Insensibly, irresistibly, our troops are following our ever-receding frontiers, and in case of a serious rising beyond the Indus, stimulated, perhaps, by Russian intrigues, this centrifugal movement would be much accelerated. Indeed, the ideal of the thorough-going, outspoken partisan of the Forward Policy, should it ever be realized, would leave the Indian Government practically without any defenders.

"When the administrative limits of India are stretched to their natural and geographical limits, the Hindu Kush," so wrote Colonel Mark Bell, in 1890, in the *Journal of the Royal United Service Institution*, "an active army of 135,000" (posted in Herat, Kandahar, Kabul, Balkh, etc.) "will be required for the defence of her scientific frontier . . . ," and "a large portion of the Indian garrison" (which is to consist nominally of 100,000 men) "would *naturally* be stationed in the Indus camps and in Pishin, and the flower of the armies of the Native princes would be actively employed

out of India."[1] Yes ; and as, at a moderate computation, every man of that vast host would cost
India twice as much on the further side of the
Indus as she pays for him on the hither side, it
would be equally "*natural*" that her inhabitants
should seize the opportunity thus wantonly con-
ceded to them, to rise against their cruel and
insane oppressors.

We are not so far yet, but provision is being
made to enable us to go so far in due season.

When the Mutiny had been suppressed, and a
Government, made wise by terrible experience, set
itself to the task of re-establishing British rule in
India on stable foundations, there was one point
on which it made up its mind without hesitation—
viz., that, for the future, the proportion between the
British and Native elements in the Anglo-Indian
army must be never less than one to two.[2] Inter-

---

[1] I suppose Colonel Bell sees his way to moving such
a vast host. Sir Henry Brackenbury, however, is evidently
of opinion that we should find it difficult to move a single
army corps, at this present moment, for field service beyond
the Frontier.—*Vide* ; his speech on the Indian Finances for
1896-97.

[2] On the 29th August, 1857, Sir John Lawrence wrote to
Mr. Colvin : "I have raised eleven regiments of Sikh Infan-

preting this decision in the spirit, as well as in the letter, Lord Canning and his Council not only increased the number of British, and diminished the number of Native troops—they also disbanded the military police, which, towards the end of the Mutiny, they had been compelled to raise; and it has been by a reversal of this latter measure that later administrations, whilst nominally respecting the proportion of one to two, have entirely destroyed that balance between the two elements in our armed forces which is essential to the security of British power in India.

In 1886 a military police was re-established— chiefly in Burma—and in 1891 began that transformation of the ordinary police into a semimilitary body, which is still going on throughout

try, and several thousand horsemen of various kinds. *I fear to raise more until I see the European troops begin to arrive from England. . . . The error we made—an error which was pointed out, but to which no one would listen—was adding to our Native troops, while the strength of the European Force actually fell off.* The insane confidence which continued vociferation on the part of our officers had generated in the fidelity of our Native army had produced a belief in England *that we could really hold India by means of these troops.*"

India. The battalions of the former force, some 19,000 strong, recruited solely from the warlike races of Northern India, commanded by British officers taken from the Indian army, armed with the breech-loader, well trained, inured to hardships, practised in jungle warfare, are already up to the level of the best of our Native troops ; and when they receive the mountain guns which are about to be issued to them, they will form the finest and most efficient fighting machine in the country—police only in name. In the latter force, since 1891, 60,000 men have been armed with the breech-loading Snider converted into smooth bores, special Reserves in all districts, with the Snider unconverted, and about 45,000 with swords ; so that, omitting these latter from the calculation, the proportion, from this single cause, stands now at less than one to three ; [1]

[1] In considering this question, it must be remembered that, in recent years, owing to the abnormally unhealthy state of the English troops in India, not less than 40 per cent. being on the sick-list and useless for war, the proper proportion between the European and Native soldiery has quite disappeared ; thus, in the Chitral Campaign it was found necessary to alter the ordinary constitution of our Anglo-Indian Division mobilized for field service, and

but other causes are at work to disturb it still further.

The forces of the Independent Native States have always been a source of danger to British ascendency in India, and it is deeply to be regretted that the statesmen, who were wise enough to cut down our own Native army, did not see their way to abolish the armies of the princes, who had either shown themselves hostile to us, or powerless to control the hostility of their soldiery. But, though they missed this great and unique opportunity of increasing our strength whilst diminishing our expenses, they

draft into each of its brigades an additional British regiment. The *Broad Arrow* of the 19th September last says that there are only some 45,000 fit for service out of a nominal strength of 70,000 men in India. Amongst other causes, to which I need not here refer, a severe epidemic of typhoid in a most virulent form has attacked the British garrison of India. Commenting on the ravages of this epidemic, *The Pioneer Mail* writes :—" We would sooner see ten lakhs spent in sterilizing filters than treble that amount devoted to mobilization arrangements,"—as " the men must be looked after, for otherwise, when the elaborate machinery for the concentration of troops is set in motion on the outbreak of war, skeleton battalions alone will be forthcoming."

at least abstained from repeating the mistake which had given to those armies their formidable character. Thenceforward there were to be no more Native contingents, drilled and led by British officers, to serve, when the latter had been got rid of, as the disciplined nucleus round which their undisciplined comrades could gather, as the bulk of Scindia's forces gathered round that Gwalior contingent which defeated General Wyndham at Cawnpur, and endangered Lord Clyde's communications, when relieving Lucknow.

Now, under the high-sounding name of Imperial Service troops, the Forward Policy has given us back those contingents, in the very heart of India, and 19,000 men, attached to us neither by natural loyalty nor by self-interest, yet equal, thanks to the exertions of their British instructors, to our best Native regiments, must be thrown into the descending scale, before we can say how far the proportion on which so much depends has really been altered for the worse ; and even then we shall have omitted the Khyber Rifles, the Frontier Militia recently re-organized, the 8,000 or 10,000 Native levies, armed at our expense, and imbued with very

fair notions of discipline by Native non-com-
missioned officers, who help to guard our North-
West Frontier, and even our communications,[1]
and the reserves of the Native army, consisting of
15,567 old soldiers "within good fighting limits
of age,"[2] whose training makes them a power,
even without the arms which at times are in
their hands.

Do not let me be misunderstood ; Native levies
are a good thing in their proper place—in front
of the position held by our troops[3]—and for their
proper work—that of keeping open the trade
routes which pass through their own lands ; a
Reserve, dwelling among a prosperous people
and sharing in their contentment, is a good thing
also, so long as it and the Native army taken
together are not permitted to assume such
proportions as to seriously outweigh their British
comrades ; and if the same condition be observed,

---

[1] In Khelat, the capital of Beluchistan, "with the aid
of a military adviser" (presumably an English officer),
"a new disciplined and efficient force was created."—
Progress and Condition of India, 1894-95.

[2] Lieutenant-General Sir Henry Brackenbury.

[3] Vide ; *India's Scientific Frontier*, page 86.

there is nothing to object to in a military police. Coupled with a policy of peace without, and development within our borders, all three may make for economy and safety ; linked to a policy of conquest without, and impoverishment within those borders, they can merely add to expenditure and insecurity. But a semi-military police is entirely evil, because less adapted than a civil force to its true duties, and because there can be no question of its taking the place of any portion of our regular Native troops ; and yet its name and its ordinary occupations hide from men the fact that it is so much added to the armed strength with which we may some day have to contend.

I am no alarmist ; I do not believe that the millions of India are burning to shake off our yoke ; but reason and experience alike assure me that the negative loyalty which is all that the vast majority of them have ever given us will not stand too hard a strain, and that dressing a man in uniform and putting a rifle in his hand does not cut him off from his own kith and kin, nor make him of the same blood and creed as ourselves, bound to us by the ties which can alone be implicitly trusted in the hour of trial.

Therefore I denounce the folly which weakens
British power in the face of a hungry people,
to whom the Indian Government persists in
offering a scientific frontier in lieu of bread.
If we are to have a Forward Policy, let it, at
least, be open and provident, avowing its aims,
and asking for what it knows it will need to
attain them—a large increase of the British army
in India. But frankness and prudence are the
last virtues that we can look for in the supporters
of that policy. They have always resorted, and
they always will resort, to every device, however
risky, rather than allow the Indian Frontier
problem to come before the British public in
its full proportions and its true colours. What
one man can do to neutralize their reticence, I
have done, and at this point I might claim
their condemnation from the sturdy good sense
of our common countrymen ; but before summing
up the facts and arguments by which I have
exposed the hollowness of the pretences on which
they have been creeping westward and northward,
and the lack of knowledge and wisdom displayed
in their military dispositions and their political
acts and calculations, I will further strengthen

my case by considering no longer what Russia's power to harm us in India might be, were she established in Afghanistan, but what it actually is, and is likely to remain.

CHAPTER IV

RUSSIA'S POSITION IN CENTRAL ASIA [1]

" Respecting Russia's right to conquer Central Asia, and England's wisdom in opposing her, much argument may be expended, and many opinions expressed ; but there is one fact which stands out beyond all controversy—the conquest of Central Asia has been a blessing, not only for Central Asia itself, but for all the nations abutting upon it."— CHARLES MARVIN.

" I have been to this region, and know what a frightful country it is for an army to traverse. . . . It is one thing for a solitary man, without baggage, to scamper over a country ; it is quite another thing for an army to traverse it, weighted with artillery, baggage, and all manner of impediments."—CAPTAIN MASLOFF, *Russian Engineers;* Author of *Skobeleff's Siege of Geok Tépé.*

" A modern army is such a very complicated organism, that any interruption in the line of communications tends to break up and destroy its very life."—LORD WOLSELEY.

THERE are two opinions held by Anglo-Indian political writers as to the causes which, in forty years' time, have brought the Russians from the Sea of Aral to the borders of Chinese Tartary,

[1] Authorities consulted for this chapter :—Captain John Wood, the first explorer of the Oxus ; Sir Henry Rawlinson ; Eugène Schuyler ; Sir Charles MacGregor ; Colonel

and from the Caspian Sea to the frontier of Afghanistan. One school of thinkers sees in this amazing advance the deliberate realization of a vast scheme of conquest conceived by Peter the Great, and never lost sight of by his successors; whilst another believes that each step forward has been taken, more or less, against the will of the Russian Government, in obedience to the necessity which compelled it to subdue one semi-savage state after another, in the search for a boundary within which it could consolidate its power and enjoy peace.

Probably there has been something of deliberate purpose, and something of accident in the phenomenon, but there is a third cause which must not be overlooked, if we would judge fairly of that phenomenon, and make sure of drawing from it sound conclusions as to its bearings on the safety of our Indian Empire—that cause the most powerful of all those which actuate the

Valentine Baker; Charles Marvin; Arminius Vambéry; C. E. Biddulph; Lieutenant-General E. Kaye; Colonel G. B. Malleson; Captain H. C. Marsh; *Times* Correspondent with the Afghan Boundary Commission; and various Parliamentary Blue Books.

B.F.   G

human race, the need, namely, of the necessaries of life—food and forage and water. Once the Russians had set foot on the great, treeless, arid plains of Central Asia, there came into play the desire to get beyond them; to reach some land where troops could, at least, be fed on the spot; and that desire has continued to operate with ever-increasing force as the conquering armies left their original source of supply further and further behind them.

When General Tchernayeff, in 1864, emerged from the desolate Kirghiz steppes, and took up a strong position on the Sir Darya, he looked to Tashkend as the desired granary; but when he had effected the capture of that city, it was only to discover that it could not support his troops, and to find himself driven to risk an immediate collision with Bokhara, by the prompt occupation of a plot of cultivated land, about twenty miles square, on the southern bank of the Chirchik, in Khokand territory, over which the first-named Khanate claimed to exercise a protectorate.

But "the rich transfluvial fields "[1] proved in-adequate to fulfil Tchernayeff's expectations, and

[1] J. M. S. Wyllie's *Essays*, p. 54.

so did Khojent, when conquered by his successor, Romanovsky, though it brought the Russians into the country lying between the Jaxertes and the Oxus, which the latter general pronounced the Garden of Central Asia. After, as before that event, and even when the culture of cotton had in many places "been abandoned for the more advantageous grain crops, the actual insufficiency of the local production was such that most of the grain for army use had to be brought from Vierny Kapal and Southern Siberia."[1] The Garden of Asia, like the fertile valleys of Afghanistan, can barely produce enough for the wants of its inhabitants, and in neither country can the soil be induced to yield much more than it does at present, for lack of the one instrument of all agricultural improvement—water.

And if supplies sufficient for the support of a small Russian army were not to be obtained in what is undoubtedly the most fertile part of Central Asia, still less have they been discovered in the barren regions, into which the Russians have penetrated on their second line of advance. The railway which starts from Usan Ada, a small

[1] Schuyler's *Turkestan*, vol. i. p. 285.

port on the Caspian Sea,[1] and ends, for the
time being, at Samarcand,[2] followed naturally
the route which offered the greatest promise of
subsistence by the way, yet for the first 144

[1] This autumn the port of Usan Ada is to be superseded by
that of Krasnovodsk, and the terminus of the Transcaspian
railway transferred to the latter place. This is the second
port which the Russians have abandoned on the eastern
coast of the Caspian Sea ; and whether they will benefit by
the present change remains to be seen, for, as Charles
Marvin tells us, "the Asiatic side of the Caspian is simply
a sandy flat with roadsteads far apart, which lie open to
every wind. Storms from the west are particularly dreaded,
and the moment the breeze begins to blow from this quarter,
the vessels stand out to sea, and remain in deep water till
it changes again."

[2] The main line is being extended to Tashkend through
a very difficult mountainous country, and a branch which
is also under construction, leaving the main line at Kho-
kent, links up Khokand and Marghilan with Samarcand,
and terminates at Andijan. The cost of Russia's railways
in Central Asia must have been enormous.   "From a
financial point of view," Mr. Charles Marvin writes, "Russia
and India have had one drawback in common in the
matter of railway construction : a large proportion of the
lines have been built for strategic purposes. But Russia
has had three other drawbacks, from which India has been
exempt.   All her railways have been badly constructed,
all of them badly financed, and all of them badly worked."

miles the view from the windows of the train, as it steams towards the south-east, chills the traveller with its lifeless monotony. On either hand, dotted here and there with stunted trees, stretch vast, unbroken plains, utterly barren and bare, except after rain, when grass springs up with extraordinary rapidity, only to fade and die away with equal suddenness—plains which, in their brief moments of vivid vitality, are the home of nomad tribes and their flocks of sheep, but, for the rest of the year, an empty desert.

Then follow, for 240 miles, separated from each other by stretches of sand, the oases of Kizil Avat, Akhal Tekke and Atak, each a long, narrow belt of cultivation, formed by numerous small streams, which streams, often dry, all descend from the mountains of Khorassan on the south-west of the oases, and lose themselves in the deserts which bound them on the north-east. Here, indeed, we have a poor, but stationary population, its narrow territories yielding barely enough for its simple wants ; and the line which brings the soldiers of the Czar into those pleasant patches of habitable land, must carry, too, all that is necessary to their maintenance. Here, again,

it is no defect in the soil which sets a limit to
the gifts of Nature ; the barren tracts on either
side the oases' belt are as susceptible of cultivation as those oases themselves, and so, too, is the
wilderness previously described ; but the water,
which could develop their latent fertility, is lacking, has always been lacking, and will continue
to be lacking to the end of the chapter. The
mountains which empty the cloud storehouse of
the monsoon, send their mighty streams southward, and only little rills trickle down their
northern declivities. It would require a Ganges
or an Indus, or both, to give Central Asia a
chance of ever rivalling India in fertility ;[1] and
though, as we are sometimes told, it may be
within the power of human science to turn the
course of the Nile, no one has ever ventured to
suggest that the Russians can compel the monsoon to blow on their side the Hindu Kush,
instead of on ours.

[1] "The two thousand miles we have marched between
the Caspian and the Indus have certainly convinced us
that India is the garden of Asia, and that only in India—
Herat and Badghis are but oases—are water and shade the
rule and not the exception."—Special Correspondent of *The
Times* with the Boundary Commission, 1885.

Beyond Atak the Transcaspian Railway crosses the Tejend River, and runs due east for 100 miles through a fresh desert to Merv ; that oasis—170 miles from the Oxus—left behind, the line takes a nearly northerly direction, and enters the country of the moving sands—firm in spring, when bound together by the grass which starts into brief existence after the melting of the snows ; at every other season, in constant motion, sweeping backwards and forwards in wild unrest, here piling up ridges, there scooping out hollows, and blowing in deadly clouds across the Oxus, whose present bed they are perpetually changing, whilst the old bed by which in former times it sought the Sea of Aral, and that by which it once flowed into the Caspian, remain as lasting memorials of their resistless might. Even the narrow railway track is only kept open by incessant vigilance and labour, and no human power can suffice to chain the Oxus to a permanent bed, or to save it from being split up into a varying number of shallow channels, which can neither be bridged nor yet navigated, except by vessels of small size and draught. The much-vaunted Russian Oxus flotilla consists of two little steamers and a few flats, none of which can carry more than 300 men. Whilst on the left bank of the Oxus the moving sands have long held undisputed sway, on its right bank their destructive activity is still at work. Beyond the narrow strip of cultivation which always marks the course of a stream, one catches glimpses, here and there, of the roofs of villages piercing the sand drifts, telling of the once fruitful soil on which only recently, perhaps, men toiled and reaped; whilst a sadder sight still are the fields in process of devastation, and the inhabited dwellings up whose walls the ruthless foe is silently creeping.

Issuing at last from this perishing region, the train pursues its way for another 236 miles to Samarcand, through the comparatively fertile valley of the Zarafshan; though, even here, constantly recurring expanses of untilled land bear witness to the paucity of water.

Now, this great railway, as I have already said, has been constructed through the least barren portion of Russia's Central Asian dominions; it follows, therefore, that the vast regions lying beyond the traveller's line of sight must be still less capable of supporting a population than those

of which he can judge from actual observation.
Mr. C. E. Biddulph, an Indian civilian, who made
the journey within the last few years, estimates
the cultivable land throughout the whole of Central Asia at 2·2 per cent., whilst the American
traveller Schuyler puts the proportion for Turkestan at $1\frac{3}{5}$ per cent. The two provinces of
Transcaspia and Turkestan, taken together, cover
1,500,000 square miles, an area only one-sixth less
than that of India and Burma combined ; but
whereas the latter countries contain 290,000,000
inhabitants, Russian Central Asia counts only
6,400,000, and this proportion of 45 to 1 can never
be altered in our rival's favour, because the limits
of India's productive power are capable of almost
indefinite expansion, whilst those of Central Asia
have practically been already reached. But the
same causes which will continue to keep down the
population in the two provinces to about its
present level, will stand in the way of any considerable addition being made to the 41,000
troops [1] of all arms of which their Russian garri-

[1] In calculating the true strength of the Russian garrison
in Central Asia, as in judging of that of the British garrison
in India, large deductions must be made for sickness.

son is now composed, and we may dismiss from
our minds the fear that Central Asia can ever be
used as a base whence to attempt the conquest
of India.

The Russians, it is true, are occupying more
and more territory, year by year, exactly as we
ourselves are doing, but the stream of advance
grows shallower as it flows, dwindling down to a
handful of men in the terrible mountain region
through which it is our latest craze to look for
their approach,[1] and if their Government is ever
mad enough to embark on the grand adventure
into which we suppose it to be burning to rush,
everything connected with that adventure—arms,
ammunition, provisions and men—must come
direct from the Caucasus, to concentrate—where?
Not at Herat, even if Herat were already in their
hands. That coveted province proves little less
disappointing than the " Garden of Central Asia "

Epidemics, at all times rife in Central Asia, have of late
years assumed most malignant forms, and the troops, as
well as the native population, have suffered and are still
suffering severely.

[1] The British members of the Commission which met last
year to delimitate the Pamirs, had to cut down their escort
to ten men, owing to transport and commissariat difficulties.

when viewed, not through the eyes of the weary,
thirst-tortured traveller, escaping with joy from
the horrors of the desert, and judging of the whole
country by the small portion of which he catches
fleeting glimpses,[1] but through those of a soldier
and diplomatist, who spent months within its
boundaries, and enjoyed unrivalled opportunities
of making himself acquainted with every part of it.

"The Herat Valley," so wrote Sir West
Ridgeway in his article on the New Afghan
Frontier, in the October, 1889, number of the
Nineteenth Century, "the Herat Valley is by no
means a smiling garden, flowing with milk and
honey. Surrounded by barren mountains, on the
lower slopes of which are a few scattered hamlets,
its central part, through which the river runs,
contains the only valuable and culturable land.
A strip on each side of the river, varying from
two to five miles in width, is fairly well cultivated,

---

[1] Vambéry's glowing vision of the future harvests of the
Badghis and Herat provinces under European rule, was
based upon the unusual number of streams by which they
are traversed. Doubtless he saw those streams full of water,
and forgot that all the smaller ones are empty, except when
the snow is melting in the mountains.

and as the villages and fields here lie close together, and the principal road runs through them,
the hurried traveller may be excused if he
generalises from what he sees, and imagines
that the whole valley is equally cultivated.
But if he were to follow one of the roads along
the outskirts of the cultivation, he would be soon
undeceived. As for fertility, if I remember rightly,
the average yield of the cultivated land is only
fivefold, or, in exceptionally fertile spots, tenfold.
Trees are few and far between, for it is a rule,
whenever Herat is threatened, to cut down every
tree within a radius of five miles. The population is poor and struggling, while Herat city
is a mass of mud hovels, sheltering some 5,000
souls, exclusive of the garrison." [1]

But were this picture as false as it is true, it
would make no difference to the solution of the

[1] "The exaggerated fears of Russian power and intrigue
entertained by Ellis, McNeil, Burnes and Wade, the flame
of which was communicated by them to the British and
Indian Governments, invested Herat with a fictitious importance wholly incommensurate with the strength of the place,
and its position in regard to Candahar and the Indus. To
speak of the integrity of the place as of vital importance to
British India was a hyperbole *so insulting to common sense*

problem I am discussing ; for, as I have pointed out, again and again, the object for which concentration is practised—viz. the massing of troops for a combined attack upon an enemy—can never, either at Herat or elsewhere, be practised by Russia in an advance upon India.

Let her push forward her railway as she may, and endow it with fourfold the carrying power which I have shown it would really possess there will yet be some point at which it must end ; that point, whatever its name, "a mere mass of mud hovels," surrounded by just as much cultivated land as will, in good years, feed its scanty population ; and beyond that point will lie mountains or desert, or both, with their inexorable refusal to permit of the passage of troops, except in very small bodies. The real truth of the situation as determined by Nature, however much delimitation commissions may trace new boundaries on their maps, is that the Asiatic Empires of

as scarcely to need refutation, and which ignorance of the countries west of the Indus, and inexperience of military operations in the East, could alone palliate."—SIR HENRY DURAND, K.C.S.I., C.B., Royal Engineers, at one time Military Member of the Viceroy's Council, and afterwards Lieutenant-Governor of the Punjab.

Great Britain and Russia practically cannot meet. Let us draw the line that is to divide them where we will, on either side of it will lie uninhabitable wastes. To put an extreme case, one which in my judgment will never occur. Supposing Afghanistan to have been entirely subdued by Russia, and that she and we have decided that our common frontier shall be drawn along the eastern foot of the Suliman Mountains—at the southern extremity of that line, *her* last outpost of any strength would be at Quetta and *ours* at Jacobabad, separated from each other by 202 miles of painful and difficult road, whilst, at its northern extremity, 81 miles of formidable passes would separate Peshawur from Jellalabad,[1] which, for argument's sake, I will assume to be as strongly fortified and garrisoned as Quetta. But when we talk of *strongly garrisoned*, we must interpret the adverb according to our experience of what can be done in that line, in a poor country, at a considerable distance from the troops' only base of supplies ; and though we may have erected at

---

[1] Jellalabad lies in the only valley of any extent between Kabul and Peshawur, and is the one spot on that route suitable for the erection of a *place d'armes*.

Quetta fortifications capable of holding 15,000 men, 3,000 to 4,000 is the maximum we are able to keep there permanently. Could the Russians do more, or anything like as much, with their true base at Tiflis, 1,748 miles away, three times farther off than ours, taking the country beyond Multan as the granary which feeds Quetta to-day ? Thus limited, neither the garrison of Quetta, nor that of Jellalabad could contribute anything to a Russian army on its march to India. Come when it may, that army must needs start from the Caucasus, and will find itself under the inexorable necessity of hurrying forward with the least possible delay. And what is the line of communication on which it would have to depend ? A single-lined railway, liable at one part of its course to be interrupted by sand, at another by snow, at a third by floods ; exposed for hundreds of miles to the danger of a flank attack from Persia (unless I am to concede that Persia, too, has become a Russian province), and for other hundreds to the raids of the Afghan tribes, who would fly to arms at once if they saw their conqueror involved in a life-and-death struggle with ourselves ; and beyond the railway, roads running

through narrow defiles, and over a waterless, burning desert—roads on which, at the very outset, the
terrible transport difficulty would be awaiting
them in the shape of endless stores, choking the
little terminus, and clamouring for camels and
mules and ponies to carry them on.

There are British officers, even British generals,
who still profess to believe that India can be in-
vaded from Central Asia ; but there are also
Russian military men who do not hesitate to
avow that such an invasion is impossible. That
very Skobeleff who, when ignorant of all the
conditions of the problem, wrote so glibly of
organizing " masses of Asiatic cavalry,[1] and hurl-
ing them into India under the banner of blood
and pillage, as a vanguard as it were, thus re-
viving the times of Tamerlane," a little later,
when his judgment had been cleared and chas-
tened by the difficulties which he had had to
overcome before he could provision and move a

---

[1] It is a curious commentary on Skobeleff's "masses of
Asiatic cavalry" that, according to Major J. Wolfe Murray,
"three very modest squadrons of irregulars, aggregating
310 rank and file, is all the Turcoman cavalry that Russia
possesses."

tiny force against the Tekke Turcomans, used very different language. " I do not understand," so he spoke to Mr. Charles Marvin, who interviewed him at St. Petersburg in 1882,—" I do not understand military men in England writing in the *Army and Navy Gazette*, which I take in and read, of a Russian invasion of India. I should not like to be the commander of such an expedition. The difficulties would be enormous. To subjugate Akhal we had only 5,000 men, and needed 20,000 camels. To get that transport, we had to send to Orenberg, to Khiva, to Bokhara, and to Mangishlak for animals. The trouble was enormous. To invade India, we should need 150,000 troops : 60,000 to enter India with, and 90,000 to guard the communications. If 5,000 men needed 20,000 camels, what would 150,000 need, and where could we get the transport ? We should require vast supplies, for Afghanistan is a poor country, and could not feed 60,000 men, and we should have to fight the Afghans as well as you." [1]

[1] Colonel Grodekoff, whom Skobeleff employed to collect supplies for the Akhal Tekke campaign, protested even more emphatically than his chief against the mischievous belief

Skobeleff might have added the factor of time to the calculation by which he turned into ridicule the scheme he himself had once favoured, and have asked, since it had taken two months to collect two and a half months' supplies for 5,000 men, and six months to bring together 20,000 camels, how many years would be needed to lay in the stores and organize the transport of 150,000 men for six, or nine, or twelve months, or any other period which might be consumed in moving them from their base to their goal? and also the factor of *wear and tear*, except that, as, in his own case, the wear and tear had amounted to the destruction of the whole of his beasts of burden, in a march of a hundred and seventy miles and a campaign of a few weeks, no increase

that Russia meditated an invasion of India, and showed at the same time a better appreciation of the resistance which the British Indian Empire could offer to its foes. "Look," he said to Mr. Marvin, "at the enormous difficulties we encountered in overcoming Geok Tepé. We killed 20,000 camels during the campaign, in which only 5,000 troops were engaged. We should need 300,000 men to invade India, and where could we obtain the transport and supplies for such a number? It would be impossible for us to march such an army to India. Rest assured that a Russian invasion of India is an impossibility."

in distance, or time could make the resultant any worse than he had found it.

That there is nothing exceptional in Skobeleff's experience will be apparent to all who remember how the whole of the transport provided for the Indian Government's grand mobilisation scheme disappeared in our own little wars, twice over, between 1889 and 1895, as well as a large proportion of the ordinary transport, as evidenced by the sums sanctioned during the same period " for additional transport mules," or "for increased purchases of transport animals to complete establishment due to casualties, etc."

The effect of this phenomenon upon the mutual relations of Great Britain and Russia is simply to render a collision between them, on any important scale, altogether impossible. Neither of them, when engaged in a hostile advance against the territory of the other, could rely exclusively, or to any great extent, upon railways. Transport, therefore, and a great deal of it, would be essential to both; and that transport, if procurable, which I dispute, must perish by thousands and hundreds of thousands on the enormous march which it would have to perform from the point where it had been collected, to the point where its services would be required by the troops, whether the original area of collection had embraced the whole of India, or the Asiatic territories of the Czar.

Of course Russia is not without her forward school of politicians, the advanced members of which are just as sanguine in their expectations, and as deaf to the teachings of experience as their Anglo-Indian rivals.

General Soboleff, for instance, considered that it ought to be as easy for his countrymen to invade India in the nineteenth century, as it was for Nadir Shah in the eighteenth, and was quite at one with Colonel Mark Bell in believing that there would be no great difficulty in maintaining a large body of troops in Afghanistan, though he wisely abstained from fixing their number, or attempting to show how they were to be supplied.[1]

[1] Colonel Bell calculates that "Afghanistan can (now) feed within its borders an armed force of 190,000 men "— (in 1838-42, and again in 1878-80, we found, to our cost, that it could not feed 10,000)—"that within five years the country could, at the most moderate computation, bear the burden of supporting 250,000 foreigners, and within ten years,

I have dealt with these fallacies so often and so fully, that there is no need to go back upon them here. My object in the present chapter has been to investigate the resources of Central Asia, viewed as the base for an invasion of India, and I think I may claim to have shown that no great force could be equipped in Turkestan, or in Transcaspia, and that we may regard the spread of Russia's power, eastward and southward, with perfect equanimity, so far as the safety of India is concerned. How we must regard her advance from the point of view of the maintenance of our authority over that country, and of our engagements to the Ruler of Afghanistan, are weighty questions which will find their place in my final chapter.

This chapter would be incomplete without a few words with regard to the province which I have accepted as Russia's base, in the conduct

500,000. *The latter figures require but* 500,000 *additional acres, or* 100 *square miles,* $\frac{1}{6000}$th *of its area of average land, to be sown with wheat!* "

The average land of Afghanistan grows nothing but rocks and stones, and he will be a clever man who can discover 500,000, or 5,000 acres of uncultivated and culturable land in its narrow valleys.

of all operations directed against Afghanistan or India, and a brief description of the army from which it is generally assumed that the troops engaged in such operations would be drawn.

The Caucasus, compared with India, is insignificant in population and resources. Its chief town, Tiflis, is connected with Baku, on the western coast of the Caspian, by a single-lined railway 341 miles long, with stations at great distances apart.

The cost of this railway, including rolling stock, was no less than £10,000 per mile ; yet the accommodation for passengers which it affords is very limited, and should it at any time be used for the conveyance of a large number of troops, with their baggage and stores, suitable vehicles would have to be provided.

Carelessly laid, the line constantly requires repairing. Last winter, for instance, so many of its bridges were destroyed by floods, that for a considerable time much of the traffic had to be carried by a circuitous route to the port of Novorosiska in Circassia. As the railway advances eastward, the region grows more and more arid, until, on approaching the Caspian, it becomes a desert, interspersed with salt-lakes, and where the heat is terrific. In this desert stands Baku, the port where the troops destined for the invasion of India would be detrained. Here rain falls so rarely that drinking water has to be brought by steamers all the way from the Volga. The passage of the Caspian occupies from twenty-four to thirty hours, and, owing to the shallow, shelving nature of the eastern shore of that great inland sea, none but small vessels of light draught can approach the quays of Usan Ada, the present starting point of the Transcaspian railway. In addition to this serious drawback, the eastern coast of the Caspian suffers, like the western, from great scarcity of water, and condensing machinery on a very large scale would have to be established there, before the first step towards an advance upon India could be taken. These preparations must prove so tedious, that, coupled with the defective character of the railway and the difficulty of disembarkation, they would almost suffice to wreck the expedition at the outset. In war, there is nothing more costly than delay, as the Russians proved in 1878–79, when the stores collected at Tchikishliar for the use of the expedition against the Turcomans of Dengeel Tepe were eaten up by the waiting troops almost as fast as they could be brought together; and the camels, arriving in twenties and thirties, had at once to be sent to the outposts to fill the gaps which death had already made in the transport train.[1]   No wonder that when the force moved at last, it was only to march to almost complete annihilation.

If on this occasion it had taken six months to provide two months' supplies for 15,000 men, and if twelve months were needed to place 25,000 men on the further side of the Caspian, how long would it take to assemble at Usan Ada the 150,000 men, with so different a transport and equipment, that would be required to attack us in India, or even the 60,000 or 70,000 which,

[1] The waste of animal life has been almost as appalling in Central Asia as in India.   In the Khiva Expedition no less than 25,000 camels were used up.   *The Golos*, referring to this terrible mortality, remarks : " It is obvious that th e people must have been almost ruined by this waste of their resources." See Marvin's *Disastrous Campaign against the Turkomans.*

with so long a line of communications to guard, would be barely sufficient to attempt the conquest of Afghanistan?

The quiet consideration of these questions must surely convince all military men that the Russian difficulties would begin on the western side of the Caspian, and an inquiry into the numbers and organization of the army of the Caucasus must still further shake their confidence in her power to enter upon undertakings of such vast magnitude, much less to carry them to a triumphant conclusion.

The estimated war strength of that army is 200,000 men and 388 guns. 70,000 of the troops belong to the Regular Army, 50,000 to the Reserve, 30,000 are Georgian and Imeritian Irregulars, and 50,000 Cossacks drawn from settlements north of the Caucasus. The 70,000 Regulars, after furnishing the garrison of Transcaspia, are distributed between Batoum, Tiflis, Kars and other fortified towns on the Turkish and Persian frontiers, whence they could not be withdrawn to take part in an invasion of India unless replaced at once by other Regulars.

The Reservists are merely military colonists,

men who after five years' service receive a grant of land, where they settle down, marry, and soon forget the little knowledge that they had acquired in the ranks, for even the regular troops are sub-jected to very light discipline, and are little better than militia.

As the 80,000 Irregulars fall, of course, far short of the standard of efficiency prevailing among the Regulars,[1] it is obvious that the Army of the Caucasus is not a very formidable force, either as regards material, discipline, or training.

But what, from our point of view, is still more satisfactory is the fact that, whether formidable or

[1] "Even the Regulars have very few parades, and abso-lutely no pipeclay. A company or two is paraded daily during the summer months for rifle practice under the Adjutant and Musketry Instructor, and the corps is assem-bled once a month for muster. The rest of the time the men do much as they choose, and usually either work at trades, selling the produce of their industry at a sort of market held every Sunday in the bazaar of the town, or hire themselves out at so much *per diem* to private individuals as porters, labourers, etc."—*Notes on the Caucasus*, by Wanderer.

These remarks, however, do not apply to the artillery, the officers of which are well trained, the men specially selected, and the guns admirably horsed and equipped.

not, it cannot safely be turned against us. Sir William Mansfield's warning to us not to forget that India was a recently conquered country, and that the commonest prudence forbade us to treat her as if she were England, for the purpose of invading Afghanistan, or of sustaining a great conflict with Russia, applies with equal force to the relations of Russia and the Caucasus. That province, also, is a recently conquered country, and its hardy, warlike inhabitants, after a struggle extending over many years, were only reduced to submission by measures of terrible severity, the memory of which must still rankle in their minds. To treat her, therefore, as though she were Russia, for the purpose of invading Afghanistan, or of sustaining a great conflict with England, would be an act of such criminal imprudence that no Russian Government is ever likely to commit it.

It comes, then, to this : that, though the food supplies of a large Russian army might be furnished by Caucasia, its *personnel* and military stores must come from Europe, which throws back its true base to the Black Sea in one direction and to Moscow in another, and deprives the dream of a Russian invasion of India of the last vestige of probability.[1]

[1] "The Russian Empire, which, from various considerations, such as its vast area, the homogeneity of its population and their stolid patriotism, is impregnable as a defensive power, is singularly weak for offence. The very qualities which make the Russian soldiery so formidable at home render them inefficient abroad. The inferior quality of the officers and generals; the indescribable corruption which makes the transport and commissariat departments invariably break down; the want of communications, and the general absence in staff and men of any intelligent spirit—these and other causes render the Russian armies, so overwhelming on paper, altogether unreliable for offensive warfare."—SIR LEPEL GRIFFIN, *Nineteenth Century*, July, 1896.

CHAPTER V

THE ALTERNATIVES

" If we engage ourselves in Afghanistan, Russia will find us in the hour of trial impoverished and embarrassed. If we keep out of Afghanistan, Russia will find us in the hour of trial strong, rich, and prosperous in India. If she really wishes us ill, she must naturally desire that we may be so infatuated as to pursue the former course. But it is for us to avoid the course which our enemies, if we have any, would desire us to follow."—SIR RICHARD TEMPLE, M.P., *formerly Member of the Viceroy's Council, and afterwards Governor of Bombay.*

" What would be an act of prudence, wisdom, and moderation at a time when we are successful, would certainly be considered by the tribes on our border as an act of weakness, if undertaken at the commencement of a war."—SIR FREDERICK (*now* LORD) ROBERTS. Memorandum, dated Kabul, May 29th, 1880, recommending the withdrawal of the British forces from Kabul, the Khyber, and the Kuram, "*within our original frontier.*"

I MAY now, at last, claim to have fully established my threefold contention—that a Russian invasion of India is impossible ; that India's present North-West Frontier is unsound and indefensible ; and that the price we are paying for the maintenance and extension of that

Frontier, is nothing less than the impoverishment of the Indian people, and the sacrifice, one by one, of the safeguards essential to the preservation of the British Indian Empire.

I have shown, firstly, that Russia possesses in Central Asia no base for the organization and supply of a large army; that the acquisition of Afghanistan would not furnish her with one, and that, consequently, she is to-day, and must continue to remain, as far off India, for all purposes of invasion, as she was when she finally established herself in the Caucasus, nearly forty years ago, except in so far as the construction of the Transcaspian Railway has increased her power of movement; that that railway, single-lined, and hampered throughout long stretches by want of water, is open for hundreds of miles to Persian attack; that, were it completed to Kandahar, or even to Kabul, it would, in its whole length, be exposed to the raids of Turcoman and Afghan, and in constant danger from sandstorm or snowstorm, earthquake or flood; and that it constitutes, therefore, too precarious a means of communication for any commander to feel himself justified in trusting to it alone;

that, if its rails were doubled, it could not relieve a Russian Government, bent on the invasion of India, of the necessity of organizing a transport train at some point or other ; that Central Asia, and Afghanistan to boot, could not supply the beasts of burden that would be required to move a force adequate to so great an enterprise ; that their numbers, were it possible to obtain them, would render the task of feeding them utterly impossible ; and that, if the transport difficulty could be overcome, and a Russian army were really to make its way through Afghanistan, there is no point within striking distance of British territory where it could halt to concentrate and recruit ; and that by whatever route it might elect to advance, by one line or many, it would always enter India in a succession of very small bodies.

I have shown, secondly, on the one hand, that the old Indus Frontier is, by nature, so exceptionally strong as to merit the epithet—invulnerable ; that its lines of communication, both lateral and in rear, are all that can be desired, and that behind it we could bring our resources to bear upon an invader with the maximum

of certainty and speed, and be in a position to
crush him at the least possible expense and loss
to ourselves, and the greatest possible expense
and loss to him; and, on the other hand, that
the new Frontier, which has replaced that of
the Indus Valley, not only lacks the advantages
attaching to the latter, but has actually trans-
formed them into dangers; that its communications are bad; that all our attempts to render
them trustworthy have failed; that the forces
by which it is held are out of proportion small
compared to the area and character of the
country, and the temper of the people[1] they
are expected to control; and that this weakness
is not accidental, but inherent in the situation—

[1] " The attitude of the population could never be depended
upon in an emergency, as was sufficiently demonstrated in
the interval between the battles of Maiwand and Kandahar,
when the very stations upon our line of rail were menaced
by bodies of marauders, and there was not a single post
throughout the whole length of our line of communications
which was not threatened or attacked in many places *in
localities where the population appeared devoted to us, and it
had been years since any sort of disturbance had occurred.*"—
MR. C. E. BIDDULPH, M.A., *Political officer with Sir
Donald Stewart's and General Phayre's forces in the Afghan
War of* 1878-79-80.

the cost of maintaining troops in a barren country at a great distance from their sources of supply, compelling the military authorities to cut down their numbers within the narrowest limits compatible with the performance of their duties under ordinary circumstances, and to allow no margin to meet emergencies.

Lastly, I have shown that the Forward Policy has added heavily to the burden of taxation borne by our Indian fellow-subjects; that it has diminished the wealth out of which taxation is paid; that it has robbed the Provincial Governments of their balances; that it has swallowed up the famine fund; that it has aggravated the exchange difficulty; that it has filled the Native Army with untrustworthy Pathans, and discontented soldiers of more loyal race; that it has destroyed that proportion between the British and Native armed forces, without which there can be no safety for our rule; and that it has increased the Independent Princes' power to injure us—in a word, that the cost of that policy has been to India the arrest of her development and the impoverishment of her inhabitants, and to Great Britain the weakening of the ties which have hitherto attached the bulk of the Indian people to her rule, and a marked decrease in her ability to cope either with civil, or military disaffection.

But if the situation which the Forward Policy has created on India's North-West Frontier is dangerously faulty, both in its external and internal aspects, what remains for reasonable men to do but to make up their minds to withdraw from it as speedily as they can? Fortunately British power in India is still strong enough to bear the strain of a retrograde movement; what we have twice safely accomplished under the pressure of immediate military and financial necessity, we can carry through a third time, of our own freewill, and in our own way, not only without danger to our authority over our legitimate subjects, but without losing the respect of the tribes, or the goodwill of the Amir.

This assertion may sound overbold, but it is easy of proof. In the first place, a return to the Indus Frontier would be in accordance with the *wishes* of all thinking and well-informed natives of India, and with the *interests* of that vast majority who, suffering ignorantly under our present Frontier Policy, would know only the results to themselves of its reversal.

In the second place, though, in virtue of our occupation of their territories, we exercise a certain control over the doings of the Independent Tribes, we are really less strong in our relations towards them than we were when we had them all in our front,[1] and commanded the

---

[1] "Apart from the question of a more formidable foe, it appears to be believed that posts pushed up the passes would lessen the chances of future contests with the unruly hill-tribes. *That they are unruly would appear an excellent reason for keeping them in our front rather than in our rear.* Posts separated by such distances and such inaccessible country can exercise no influence on the inhabitants between ; on the contrary, we should be offering them new and potent means of molesting us. I fear that slenderly escorted convoys would offer irresistible temptations to the half-starved hill-tribes. *Such a measure, in time of war most mischievous as multiplying chances of disaster, would be in time of peace costly and burthensome, for it would not in the least obviate the necessity of keeping up our present line of Frontier guards."*—SIR EDWARD HAMLEY *on India's North-West Frontier.*

The Indian Government has just decided to strengthen the garrisons of the old Frontier stations referred to by Sir E. Hamley.

mouths of the passes by which they must issue forth, if they wanted to meddle with us ; and they are quick-witted enough to be aware that, in returning to our former position, we should forfeit none of our ability to punish them for bad behaviour, and to reward them for good ; wise enough to know that they would still be in *our* hands, we no longer in *theirs*.[1]

In the third place, though we occupied the

---

[1] "Cases of Ghazism (*i.e.* murder) along the Zhob Valley, and further along the Frontier, have been numerous of recent years. . . . The moment one of these crimes has been committed on our side of the Frontier, the culprit immediately escapes with all speed over the boundary into Afghanistan, where he finds himself in a sanctuary. . . . For months on end our officers, both civil and military, are stationed at forts entirely cut off from communication with the world to which they belong, deprived of all means of amusements, in an intolerable climate, with very little physical comfort, and compelled in many places to the accompaniment of an escort whenever they get a mile from their station."—*See ;* SIR JOHN DICKSON-POYNDER'S article in the *National Review* for September last, also *India's Scientific Frontier*, pp. 62 and 63.

Since Sir John Dickson-Poynder's visit to the North-West Frontier, the Government of India have prohibited officers and others travelling in these disturbed districts " without special permission of local political authorities."

territories of the Independent Tribes with the Amir's consent, and the step was represented to him as essential to the success of our plan for the protection of his dominions against the ambitious designs of Russia, there is no doubt that that consent was most reluctantly given, that Abdur Rahman feels aggrieved by the substitution of our influence for his over men of Afghan blood, and that he sees in our establishment on the borders of Afghanistan a grave and constant menace to the integrity of that kingdom.[1] So far, then, from viewing our retirement with disfavour, he would welcome it as the most convincing proof that we could offer him of our friendly intentions towards him and his people.

I shall probably be told that Abdur Rahman yielded to our wishes in regard to the Independent Tribes in exchange for a promise of armed

---

[1] The *Times of India* draws attention to the fact that "The Government of India are by no means at the end of their trouble with the Ameer over the Mohmand question," and that "it is becoming apparent that Afghan influence is being extended over the Eastern clans right up to the border of Michni," where the Kabul River leaves the hills and enters into the Peshawar Valley.

assistance in the event of a Russian violation of his frontier, and that he will be reluctant to relinquish that promise. Personally, I believe that Russia would find it harder to establish herself in Afghanistan than we did ; that the Amir is quite capable of fighting his own battles against her; and that he is far less afraid of her than of us. But granting that the Amir really shares our dread of Russia, and values the pledge of British assistance given to him on his accession to the throne, in 1880, and, probably, renewed in 1893—there was nothing in the terms of that pledge, at least as originally worded, to bind us to give that assistance in any particular form, certainly nothing to prevent our placing ourselves in a better position for the keeping of our promises by retiring from territories which we occupied long after they were made.

To attempt to oust the Russians from Herat —supposing them to have occupied that city—by marching an Anglo-Indian army hundreds of miles through Afghan territory, with the certainty of embroiling ourselves with the people whom we had come to aid, would be no less futile than dangerous ; and yet that is exactly what

we are sure to do, or to attempt to do, if New
Chaman and Quetta are still in our hands. To
make no use of positions for which India has
had to pay so high a price, when the occasion of
turning them to account had presented itself,
would seem culpable waste, and only experience
could convince the partisans of the Forward
Policy that the possession of these stepping-
stones would do little to facilitate the attainment
of their distant goal, and not much to diminish
the immediate expense of reaching it, since the
personnel and supplies of the expeditionary force
would still have to be brought direct from India.

No!—there is only one way of helping
Afghanistan without arousing her jealousy, and
probably in the end justifying her suspicions, and
that is to tell Russia that we intend to regard
any act of aggression committed against the
territory of our ally as an act of hostility
directed against ourselves, and to avenge it by
attacking her in her only vulnerable points—her
sea-board, her commerce, and her fleet.[1]

[1] "No railways, no forts, no agreements are of the least
use unless the English Government—I do not mean the
Government of to-day or to-morrow—unless the English

By adopting this course we should add to the
three lines of defence already protecting our
Indian Empire on the north-west, yet a fourth,
in the shape of a truly friendly Afghanistan; and
in case of a war with Russia, and perhaps some
other European power, so far from having to
increase the strength of India's British garrison,
we could draw boldly upon her Native troops
to meet dangers threatening us in Eastern Asia,
or Africa.

The probabilities, however, are strong that a
clear declaration of our intentions, made openly
in the face of the world, would suffice to safe-
guard the integrity of Afghanistan. Russia may
covet Herat, but she is little likely to provoke
us to war for the sake of adding a few more
thousand unprofitable square miles to the millions
which she already possesses in Central Asia—
totally unprofitable, from a military point of
view, because, though portions of the Herat
Valley are of average fertility, they are far too

Government, supported by the voice of the people, insist
that Russia shall no more cross the Afghan frontier than
that her troops should land on the coast of Kent or
Sussex."—SIR LEPEL GRIFFIN.

limited in extent to solve the problem of supply-
ing the needs of an army on the long march to
India. And if, as some Anglo-Indian statesmen
believe, Russia's restless activity on one side of
the Hindu Kush is prompted by fear of us, as
our equally restless activity on the other side is
prompted by fear of her—is it not clear that we
could take no step better calculated to allay her
anxiety, and to induce her to abstain from giving
the Amir of Afghanistan any just cause of
offence, than our own withdrawal from the borders
of his kingdom?

But whether Russia's forward policy is, or is
not, dictated by fears as unreasoning as our own,
and whether her eyes are, or are not, capable of
being opened to the ruinous folly of the rivalry
between herself and us in regions where each
country is safe within its own limits, and cannot,
if it would, overstep the other's boundary, matters
little; what does matter is that Great Britain
should abandon and disavow her own Forward
Policy, and should reap the advantages of a return
to wiser counsels, not in India alone, but wherever
her influence and her interests extend, that is
to say, in every quarter of the globe.

The first of these advantages will be the power to reduce India's ruinous military expenditure ; the second, the power to place her military system on a safe and efficient footing—safe and efficient, because the due proportion between her British and Native armed forces could be at once restored ; because the Pathans in the Native army would cease to be dangerous, when free from the temptation to betray us to their own kith and kin ; because the discontent which service out of India and in unhealthy localities [1] never fails to awaken in the breasts of Hindu and Mahomedan, Sikh and Goorkha, would disappear from that army when such service would

[1] According to information which has appeared, from time to time, in the Indian papers, our forces in Beluchistan, Chitral, and the Malakand Pass are all abnormally sickly, and the mortality among them very high. In connection with this point it is well to recall the fact that, in 1880, Lord Roberts advocated "withdrawing all, or nearly all, the European troops from Peshawur, and reducing the garrison to the lowest possible strength," on the ground that we could only ensure "a healthy and serviceable force, fit to take the field at any period of the year," by keeping our troops, as an ordinary thing, under favourable conditions. "Only persons," so he wrote, "who live amongst soldiers know the effect of quartering them in unhealthy places."

no longer be required of it, except under exceptional circumstances and for short periods of
time,[1] and because when we ceased squandering
India's money on useless fortifications and railways, unstable as water, we should be able to
increase the pay of our Native troops,[2] and to
endow every Native regiment with a full comple-
ment of British officers.[3]

[1] "The condition, welfare, and loyalty of the Native
Army must always be important factors in determining
questions of Indian foreign policy."—Memorandum from
Sir FREDERICK ROBERTS, dated Kabul, 29th May, 1880.

[2] The present Commander-in-Chief in India, Sir George
White, has secured for the Native Army an increase of
pay, but it is still underpaid. A table servant in India
often gets a higher wage than a Sepoy, whose contributions to regimental funds are not inconsiderable, and who,
unlike our English soldiers, has generally a wife and
family to maintain.

[3] "The greatest want, in my opinion, and, I know, in
the opinion of the Commander-in-Chief, is an increase to
the number of British officers in the Indian Army. We
have endeavoured to meet this by establishing a reserve
of officers, but the attempt has been a failure. . . . Yet
upon the outbreak of war we ought to increase the number
of European officers with every unit of the Native Army,
and we should require some hundreds of officers for
transport duties and various staff appointments in the
field. Where to lay hands upon these officers is a problem

The third advantage to be reaped from a reversal of our recent Frontier Policy will be the opportunity it will afford us of ridding ourselves of that gratuitously created danger—the Imperial Service Troops;[1] and of bringing moral pressure to bear upon the Independent Princes to induce them to cut down their overgrown and utterly useless armies. When we can say with conviction, no danger threatens India, from without, that our troops are not perfectly well able to meet, we shall be justified in showing the displeasure with which we view the continued maintenance of forces that have no legitimate *raison d'être*, and which each prince keeps up to be ready to take advantage of any failure of our power. I need hardly say that the princes whom we should ask to sacrifice their military pride, or their secret

that has not been solved. Should the finances of India improve, I earnestly hope that this question will not be lost sight of."—SIR HENRY BRACKENBURY, *late Military Member Viceroy's Council.*

[1] The maintenance of the Imperial Service Troops costs annually no less than Rs. 5,784,910, of which the Indian Government contributes Rs. 200,000. The people who have to provide this large sum are already more heavily taxed than our own subjects.

ambitions, to the welfare of the whole Indian people—their own subjects would be the first to profit by the change—would, as civil rulers, deserve redoubled consideration at our hands, and that we could afford to leave them greater freedom in the management of the internal affairs of their States, when relieved ourselves of the fear that that freedom might some day be used to jeopardise the peace of which we are the guardians. When armies, which now amount to 401,850 men with 6,150 cannon,[1] have been cut down to the numbers required for ceremonial purposes, and a properly organized police has taken their place in each Native State, India might reap yet another advantage in the shape of a reduction of her own army, a large proportion of which is at present engaged in keeping a watch upon the movements of these independent forces.[2] Relieved from that duty, 150,000 Native

---

[1] " Taking both regular and irregular troops together, the estimated total strength of the force in 1891–92 was 324,670 infantry, 77,180 cavalry, and 6,150 guns."—*Moral and Material Progress in India*, 1891–92.

[2] The following troops are employed in watching the armies of the Independent States :—14,000 British Troops, 18,000 Native Troops, and 114 guns.

troops would no longer be required to guard her borders and preserve her internal peace, and a reduction in their numbers would justify the British Government in proportionally reducing those of their British comrades.[1]

This last reduction would bring with it a fifth advantage, since by reducing the home charges, so irksome to the Indian Government, it would make an appreciable difference to it in the matter of exchange.

Yet another advantage would be the ability to re-occupy strategical points of vastly greater importance to the safety of India and of India's Government than Quetta—points which of late years have been abandoned, or stinted of troops to satisfy the demands of the North-West Frontier.[2]

[1] "A standing army which is larger than is necessary for home requirements will be a tempting and almost an irresistible weapon of offence beyond the border."—SIR AUCKLAND COLVIN.

[2] "In Nepaul we have to deal with a potential danger of more than ordinary significance. In some respects it may be compared to Afghanistan ; but, both in position as regards our own territory and in union among them-selves, the Nepaulese must be considered as being more formidable than the Afghans.

"While our whole military system has been adapted

And one and all of these changes would lead directly up to a diminution of taxation and an increase in the material well-being of the Indian people.

Economy, security, prosperity—these would be India's gain, and Great Britain would share these blessings with her and earn yet others for herself ; viz., *in India*—an assured political position, resting on the contentment of the great rural class, which, in that country, numbers 80 per cent. of the entire population, entrenched in which she could face with tranquil mind the great problem of how to reconcile her rule with the satisfaction of the legitimate aspirations of the educated native ; *at Home*—freedom to base her conduct towards other nations on her principles, rather than on

to insure the security of the North-West Frontier, very slight preparations have been made towards repelling attack from Nepaul. Should the Goorkhas ever produce a great leader, without the prudence or the other distrac-tions of Jung Bahadur, the peril would assume a more tangible form than, fortunately, it can be said to possess at present.

" Then it would be recalled that the Khatmandhu Court had striven to form and head a league of the princes of India against us in 1839."—" The Armies of the Native States of India." (Reprinted from *The Times*, 1885.)

her apprehensions. Can any reasonable man doubt that it would be easier and safer to admit some of our Indian fellow-subjects to a larger share in the administration of their country, if we had broken with a policy by which all are impoverished and many exasperated ? or question that our influence in Europe would be doubled if it were known to all its Governments that— having ceased to strain India's resources to the uttermost in guarding against imaginary dangers, and having strengthened our hold upon the good- will of her people and the loyalty of her army— we could enter into war, should war be forced upon us, unhampered by the fear of being suddenly called upon to meet some great emer- gency, 10,000 miles from our shores?

There are men who will talk of the loss of prestige involved in the step I counsel, but no nation's prestige can suffer from an accession of strength ; and if ours were to decline temporarily, in the eyes of such of our neighbours as should fail to see what we gain by a withdrawal from Beluchistan and Waziristan, from Gilgit and Chitral, the mistake might injure them, but could not injure us. Such a step would, indeed, be a confession of past ignorance and folly, but then it would, at the same time, be a proclamation of a return to knowledge and common sense. Certainly, as a people, we have not been in the habit of living by the applause and admiration of our neighbours, but by the robust determination to go our own way, and we may be glad, in this case, that we are strong enough to take it. A small nation may sometimes be tied and bound by its own mistakes; a great nation can break through them and live them down, and *that* in an incredibly brief time. The world's memory is of the shortest, and no practical politician troubles his head about yesterday's errors, or yesterday's successes; he has enough to do in grappling with the errors, and ensuring the successes of to-day. Even in India, the reckless extravagance of the last decade would soon be forgotten. It is this year's taxation, not last year's, which galls and embitters; the road, the bridge, the canal, which the peasant sees growing under his eyes, soon efface from his mind the length of time that he has had to wait for them. Let us thank God for this happy gift of forgetfulness, and profit by it to regain, as

B.F.   K

quickly as possible, the character of beneficent rulers, which we once possessed, and of late have forfeited.

Other critics will accuse me of taking no thought for British trade, of which it is our boast that it everywhere follows the British flag. But what is the trade of the 78,000 square miles which the Forward Policy has added to the British Empire, compared to the trade which might be ours were India rich and progressive, instead of poor and stationary? Three hundred millions of people as against, perhaps, one and a half million! The former at our doors, for the sea is no barrier between them and us; the latter, far away and difficult to reach! The former inhabiting a land to which irrigation can bring constantly increasing fertility; the latter scattered over mountains and deserts, which defy the power of man to change their character! If one market is to be sacrificed to the other, which, I ask, is the better worth preserving?

But there is no occasion to choose between them. Trade passes safely through the Khyber, with the consent of the subsidised Khyber tribes and under the protection of the Khyber levies, and there is no reason why the same inexpensive arrangements should not keep every other trade route safe and open. The cost would be a trifle when weighed against the sums now wasted on railways and roads, which crumble under the hands of their builders.

But bad as our present position on this frontier may be, it is safe and economical compared to that which must eventually succeed it, if we persist in remaining where we are. I know I shall be told that, whatever irresponsible members of the Forward school may write about pushing forward our posts to the northern side of the Hindu Kush, the Indian Government has no intention of encroaching upon the dominions of the Amir. I do not question the sincerity of its desire to avoid involving India in a third Afghan War; what I contend is that circumstances must some day, may any day, prove too strong for its intentions.

So long as the deep belt of territory occupied by the Independent Tribes lay between Afghanistan and India, it was possible for the former country to be torn and vexed for years together by internecine strife, without that strife's giving

rise to any incident that called for our inter-
ference ; and when one prince, stronger than the
rest, at last succeeded in establishing himself on
the throne of Kabul, there was nothing to prevent
our entering at once into friendly relations with
his Government. But no such belt now separates
the two States, and when confusion and lawlessness
next reign in Afghanistan—as reign they almost
certainly will when the stern hand, which now
keeps order there, is withdrawn—violations of
our Frontier are sure to occur. These will have
to be repressed and punished ; and once we are
brought into collision with any section of the
Afghan people, the chances are small of our being
able to escape taking sides with one or other
of the contending factions ; the side we espoused
would become the anti-patriotic side, and all the
difficulties and dangers of the first Afghan War
would at once confront us. As, under existing circumstances, the Russians would be certain to lend
their aid to the opposite side, those difficulties and
dangers, far from being less than on the former
occasion, would be greatly multiplied, and our
expenditure in men and money correspondingly
increased. But where is the money, and where

are the men to come from? Has not the present
Secretary of State for India admitted that there
is no new tax which the Indian Government could
impose, no possibility of extracting more revenue
out of existing taxes? and is it not disgracefully
true that the richest Provincial Government, that
of Bengal, has been driven, for lack of funds, to
revert to such vexatious and long since condemned imposts as a sliding scale of taxation on
wedding expenditure, fees on religious ceremonies,
a tax on village carts, and tolls upon bridges and
roads? As for the men, we have only to recall
the fact that eighteen months after the beginning
of the last Afghan War recruiting had practically
ceased in India,[1] and to realize that a third
Afghan War would be highly unpopular, from the
beginning, with an army which has not yet had
time to forget the fatigues and hardships of the
second—to feel sure we could not count upon
obtaining all we should need.

But short of money and short of men, what

[1] "In case of a prolonged campaign recruiting might
fail, as happened in the last Afghan War."—Extract de-
spatch from the Government of India to the Secretary of
State, 14th August, 1885.

could the Indian Government do but adopt, a few
years hence, under compulsion, the very course
on which I would have it enter freely to-day?
a course which, safe and honourable now, would
then be fraught with peril and shadowed by
disgrace.

Intentions are worthless when circumstances are
beyond men's control, and that circumstances on
the North-West Frontier are beyond the control
of the Indian Government is due to the fact that
it has chosen to draw that frontier where nature
never intended it to be. Let us then reclaim our
freedom of action whilst there is yet time—
freedom to do our full duty by the people of
India ; freedom to show ourselves firm, but kindly,
neighbours to the Independent Tribes ; freedom
to keep our oft-repeated promises to respect the
independence and integrity of Afghanistan ; freedom to smile at Russia's threats, whilst removing
her legitimate grounds of anxiety ; freedom to
guide our policy all the world over by our sense
of right and justice.

It is no untried experiment I advocate, no
purely visionary gains that I dare to foretell.

That experiment has already been put to the

THE ALTERNATIVES 135

test with just such results as I have a right to
expect of it were it to be repeated to-morrow.

When Lord Ripon arrived in India, in June,
1880, he found the Anglo-Indian army occupying
the whole of Afghanistan. Within one year from
that date, India, except for the retention of Quetta
and the Pishin Valley, had returned to her old
frontier,[1] and the Government of India, every
member of which loyally supported the new order
of things, could turn its attention to the task of
undoing the evil work of the previous administration. In 1881–82, 82–83, 83–84, the military
expenditure was brought down to a point not
greatly exceeding the standard prevailing before
the war, while in 1884–85 it was Rs. 760,664 below
that standard ; and yet Sir Auckland Colvin, the
then Financial Member of Council, was able to
state that although " the total net military charges
in India and England were lower than they had
been at any time during the past ten years, this
had been effected without prejudice to efficiency,
or any reduction in the authorized aggregate
strength of the army, and notwithstanding that
the non-effective and superannuation charges have

[1] See ; *India's Scientific Frontier*, p. 51.

in recent years largely increased."[1] Careful husbanding of the Indian finances gave, by the end of the financial year 1883–84, an Imperial surplus of revenue over expenditure of Rs. 13,874,960; but Lord Ripon did not wait to have this sum in hand before entering upon important fiscal and domestic reforms.

The salt tax was largely reduced, and the whole of the import duties, with the exception of those on wine, spirits, malt liquor, arms and ammunition, were abolished. The borrowing of money for the construction of railways was continued, but under strict compliance with the principle laid down by Lord Hartington, that *no new line was to be undertaken unless the prospects of its proving remunerative were good.*

Fresh contracts were entered into with the Provincial Governments, each of which was started on its new career with a substantial sum in hand, whilst all were encouraged, in their turn, to economize and develop their resources, by the assurance that the Central Government would not rob them of the fruit of their self-denial and energy.

[1] *Indian Financial Statement for* 1885–86.

Lastly, the famine fund, of which mention has several times been made in these pages, was established on a permanent footing, not only to relieve existing distress, but to carry out the public works by which the danger of famine's occurring could gradually be lessened, if not entirely overcome.

And what were the political results of the withdrawal from Afghanistan—the Afghanistan of the Tribes, as well as the Afghanistan of the Amir? Did it produce alarm and disaffection in India? Did it mortify and discontent the Native Army? Did it lower our influence with the Independent Tribes and encourage them to raid upon our territory? Did it weaken us in our relations to our European neighbours?

The answer to every one of these questions is an emphatic—No. The Indian people, relieved from the strain of war, went about its ordinary occupations with renewed activity and cheerfulness. The Native Army rejoiced to find itself once more at home. The Independent Tribes respected our border so scrupulously that, during the whole of Lord Ripon's administration, not a single punitive expedition had to be sent against

them, and the British Government could embark
on the Egyptian and Soudan campaigns without
any fear of being called upon to strengthen our
forces in India.   On the contrary, the Indian
Government was able to lend troops to Great
Britain, and even to contribute Rs. 6,820,000 to the
expenses of the Egyptian War, and this without
having to impose fresh burdens on its subjects.

The good conduct of the tribes is, of course,
susceptible of the explanation that in the Afghan
War we had so broken and cowed them,
that they dared not provoke us afresh ; but
looking to all the facts of the Frontier situation
both then and since, it seems attributable, rather,
to our return to a position in which experience
had long taught them that they could effect
nothing against us, and to Lord Ripon's honourable abstention from all action that could alarm,
or trouble them.

But if four short years, under the guidance of
men whose hearts were set upon making British
rule in India strong in the only durable way,
sufficed to undo all the harm that had been
wrought during those other four years, in which
the Forward Policy had been in the ascendant,

(except, indeed, to give back the lives and money which had been thrown away)—what might not the eleven years, which have since elapsed, have done to add to India's prosperity and contentment, had the Government continued to move forward in the path of peace, economy, and quiet confidence in its own strength?

But, unfortunately, with the expiration of Lord Ripon's term of office, our Frontier Policy once more suffered reversal. The Penjdeh incident, which occurred shortly after Lord Dufferin's arrival in India, was the immediate cause of the change; but that incident in the hands of men free from illusions with regard to Russia's power to harm us, and strong to resist the ambitious promptings of the military clique to whose influence the Government of India is ceaselessly exposed, would never have been exalted into the rank of an event of first-class importance. As things were, the scare which it excited could hardly have been greater if, instead of a skirmish between Russians and Afghans, 600 miles from our most advanced post, the Russians had been knocking at the gates of Peshawur.

Rs. 22,880,710 of India's money disappeared in

war preparations alone before that scare wore itself
out. Wear itself out it did, in the end, but it left
behind a spirit which has never since ceased to
dominate Indian affairs, and to which are attributable all the ills set forth in the second chapter
of my previous volume, and the first three chap-
ters of this one. More quickly than good had
effaced evil, evil, once more triumphant, wiped
out good.

It seems to me, that the one weak point in Lord
Ripon's Frontier Policy is responsible for this disastrous change of front. Had we fallen back at the
southern extremity of the North-West Frontier as
completely as we fell back on its northern extremity, a fresh advance, beginning *ab ovo*, would
have presented itself to the Government of India
and to public opinion, both there and here, in its
full magnitude, and would have met with wide
discussion and weighty opposition. But Quetta
and Pishin[1] retained, made that "insidious

[1] Quetta, though not Afghan territory, had been occupied
by Lord Lytton as a first step towards the invasion of
Afghanistan ; and his successor might have well included
its abandonment in the settlement by which he sought to
restore good feeling between the Afghans and ourselves.
As regards Pishin, many eminent statesmen and soldiers

method of creeping over the country like a mist,"
so indignantly repudiated by Sir William Mansfield, possible and easy.

Month by month, our posts moved farther away
from their supports ; month by month, the expense
of keeping them supplied with food and munitions
of war grew greater ; month by month, the military frontier railways swallowed up lakhs of rupees
and holocausts of lives—and yet, outside a narrow
military and civil official circle, no one knew what
was going on ; and when the financial difficulties,
which were the inevitable fruit of such reckless
expenditure, became too glaring for concealment,
the fall in exchange came to the help of the
military authorities as a scapegoat on whose back
to lay the burden of their own sins.

Therefore it is that I put no faith in any partial retirement. Even if it were not palpably as
wise a thing " to let the web of difficulties " spread
itself for our enemies to the mouth of the Bolan
as to the mouth of the Khyber ; even if Quetta
and its communications were not a financial quick-
sand in which millions of rupees must annually

were in favour of giving it back to the Amir—Lord Wolseley
for one.

disappear to no purpose—I should still urge the abandonment of that fortress, on the ground that we should never be safe against the temptation to use it as a base whence to renew our conquests. I am not blind to the fact that there are at Quetta great works, both military and civil, the relinquishment, or destruction of which would appear to entail immense loss on the State which created them ; but, as a matter of fact, works which serve no good end, by which India is not, and never will be, the richer, or the safer, are in themselves a dead loss to that State, a loss which the cost of maintaining them renders heavier year by year ; and the charge of culpable waste must be brought, not against those who would abandon, but against those who would retain them.

I have said that the memory of nations is short, and that we may well be thankful that this is the case ; but that faculty of forgetfulness has its bad as well as its good side, and the British Public, distracted by a thousand contending interests and anxieties, must, of necessity, dismiss one subject from its mind to make room for another. Even if I could convert the entire Press and People of England to my views to-day, their hold on the facts and reasonings by which that conversion would have been effected, would be so weak that, a very few years hence, they would be unable to recall them, and timid or ambitious men might once again appeal, not in vain, to their fears, or their patriotism, for leave to plunge India back into the slough of despond from which she had escaped.

My Policy, therefore, is " Thorough." Of all our useless possessions let us keep not a single square mile to tempt us to our hurt ; but resolutely shutting the book of aggression and extravagance, let us open that of internal development and economy. And let this be done, not in secret, but openly, that all the world may know that we have returned to our right mind, and that in regaining wisdom we have bought back strength.

Butler & Tanner, The Selwood Printing Works, Frome, and London.

Opinions of the Press.

CAN RUSSIA INVADE INDIA?

BY

COLONEL H. B. HANNA.

Saturday Review.—"We recommend those who wish to make a closer acquaintance with the Indian frontier problem to read a book by Colonel H. B. Hanna, *Can Russia Invade India ?* "

Tablet.—"We recommend this book to all who are scared by the bugbear of Russian advance in Central Asia. . . . Colonel Hanna's powerful pamphlet will remain as a powerful contribution to an important subject from one whose military knowledge and personal experience give him a right to be heard as an expert."

Westminster Gazette.—"An excellent little book likely to be extremely useful. All who can read words of two or more syllables, and all free libraries and political clubs, should have *Can Russia Invade India ?* on their shelves."

The Speaker.—"Since the military alarmist, in one form or another, is ever with us, the appeal to cool judgment and common sense is never superfluous."

Broad Arrow.—"He writes with an intimate topographical knowledge of his theme, and we are impressed with a consciousness that the financial condition of India imperatively forbids an adventurous policy which cannot be justified by a clear demonstration that he is wrong."

Asiatic Quarterly Review.—"Our gallant author's painstaking book should be read by all who have at heart the maintenance of the Empire ; for it shows admirably at least one side of the vital question, which should be studied from each of its several points of view."

Manchester Guardian.—"Colonel Hanna, a soldier of experience and distinction, with a personal knowledge of the North-West Frontier, takes one by one the routes by which it has been thought possible that India might be attacked on that side, and works out carefully the time that would be required for Russian troops to reach the British posts on, or near the Indus, the force that would be necessary to make a successful attack possible, and the supplies that would be needed to bring it alive through the deserts beyond our old frontier. The result is a demonstration unanswerable, as far as we can now see, of the absolute impracticability of such an enterprise."

Times of India.—" Colonel H. B. Hanna, Bengal Staff Corps, gives a very lucid and unbiassed statement of the problem and the reasons which convince him that, by whatever political move Russia may seek to embarrass us in Central Asia, the actual invasion of India is known by the Russian Government to be now almost impossible. With these conclusions we are in entire sympathy. . . . The impossible dies hard, as we all know, but here is a task which is almost outside the realms of the thinkable."

Indian Spectator.—" With regard to one great question of the day—the wasting of India's reserves beyond her frontiers—there is a small book that should be mentioned, by . . . Colonel H. B. Hanna, entitled *Can Russia Invade India?* For those who have any capacity to understand physical geography and the exigencies of military supply and transport it shows that Russia can't, could not, if she would."

ARCHIBALD CONSTABLE & CO.,

2, WHITEHALL GARDENS, S.W.

Sold by all Booksellers.

Opinions of the Press.

INDIA'S SCIENTIFIC FRONTIER.

WHERE IS IT? WHAT IS IT?

BY

COLONEL H. B. HANNA.

Manchester Guardian.—"Colonel Hanna has given in a comparatively small space and with admirable clearness such a conspectus of recent frontier policy in India as can hardly be found elsewhere, and such a demonstration of its real meaning and too probable consequences as should have an effect, even at this eleventh hour, on every mind not obstinately closed against conviction."

Saturday Review.—" Colonel Hanna is well known in India, where he saw much service and acquired the reputation of an active and sagacious officer. He is personally acquainted with the character and quality of the several classes from which our native Indian army is recruited. He has campaigned beyond the frontier, and took part in the last Kabul war. He writes with competent knowledge of his subject, and is entitled, therefore, to impartial hearing."

Scotsman.—" Colonel Hanna's new tract on *India's Scientific Frontier* is a piece of trenchant criticism, and a most powerful protest against the forward policy now in the ascendant on our Indian frontier. . . . Looked at from a purely literary point of view, this is a powerfully written pamphlet, vigorous in style, and strong both in facts and arguments."

Liberal.—" We would once more call attention to the great value of the series called 'Indian Problems,' which Colonel H. B. Hanna is at present publishing. To all desirous of gaining an acquaintance with the *pros* and *cons* of our Indian frontier question no authorities can be named better than these little *brochures*. They are the most authoritative pronouncements on the subject we yet have had. They trace the progress of the frontier question from 1876 until the present day, and collect a large amount of most interesting and valuable matter not otherwise easily accessible.

Colonel Hanna is an impartial controversialist. Though one can see which way his sympathies turn, he is as ready to praise Conservative statesmanship when it is deserving of praise as he is to reflect on Liberal blunders when they merit animadversion. The little books form the best handbooks of their kind on the Indian frontier question."

Bombay Gazette.—"Colonel Hanna has rendered even a greater service to his countrymen than by his previous pamphlet, *Can Russia Invade India?* . . . In his second pamphlet Colonel Hanna points out how hopeless have been the struggles and how endless the expenditure occasioned us by the pursuit of a Scientific Frontier, which, dancing about before our eyes like a will-of-the-wisp, has led us now to Kandahar, now to Chitral, and again to Kurram and Waziristan. There is reason to fear that it will end by leading us into difficulties and dangers from which we shall find it more and more impossible to extricate ourselves, unless reason steps forward and puts an end to the chase."

Guardian.—"This is a powerful argument in favour of the Lawrence policy. . . . It is always useful to have both sides of a disputable position clearly and forcibly stated, and we probably have in this book the very strongest case that can be made out for the policy of 'masterly inactivity.' "

The Champion.—"A book worth reading. . . . As a general rule, books written by military men upon matters of state-craft are of little importance. Soldiers seem unable to take a broad view of anything outside their own profession, and, consequently, not much heed is taken of their political ideas. It is, therefore, with pleasurable surprise that we welcome the literary work of Colonel H. B. Hanna."

Literary World.—"The forward policy is in the ascendant for the present, the Government in power having pronounced against the decision of Lord Rosebery's Cabinet to withdraw entirely from Chitral. But perhaps a day will come when Colonel Hanna's vaticinations of disaster will be justified by events."

Christian World.—"This is an exhaustive and very able examination of the whole question."

Glasgow Herald.—"Colonel Hanna's book is a valuable and clearly written repertory of facts, and forms a useful addition to a reference library. . . . Colonel Hanna states his views with great clearness and ability."

ARCHIBALD CONSTABLE & CO.,

2, WHITEHALL GARDENS, S.W.

Sold by all Booksellers.

CONSTABLE'S
Hand Atlas of India

A NEW SERIES of Sixty Maps and Plans
prepared from Ordnance and other Surveys
under the direction of

J. G. BARTHOLOMEW, F.R.G.S.,
F.R.S.E., &c.

In half morocco, or full bound cloth, gilt top, 14s.

This Atlas is the first publication of its kind, and for
tourists and travellers generally it will be found particularly
useful. There are Twenty-two Plans of the principal towns
of our Indian Empire, based on the most recent surveys,
and officially revised to date in India.

The Topographical Section Maps are an accurate reduction of the Survey of India, and contain all the places
described in Sir W. W. Hunter's "Gazetteer of India,"
according to his spelling.

The Military, Railway, Telegraph, and Mission Station
Maps are designed to meet the requirements of the Military
and Civil Service, also missionaries and business men who
at present have no means of obtaining the information they
require in a handy form.

The index contains upwards of ten thousand names, and
will be found more complete than any yet attempted on a
similar scale.

Further to increase the utility of the work as a reference
volume, an abstract of the 1891 Census has been added.

"It is tolerably safe to predict that no sensible traveller will go to
India in future without providing himself with 'Constable's Hand Atlas
of India.' Nothing half so useful has been done for many years to help
both the traveller in India and the student at home. 'Constable's Hand
Atlas' is a pleasure to hold and to turn over."—*Athenæum.*